The Sacred Stone

KAREN I SAGE

Cover design by: Art Painter

Cover background image: 'Electric Sky'

Copyright © Darryl Reid

nlightimages.com

CONTENTS

THE NORTHERN LIGHTS

Glowing green ribbons of light swayed across the midnight sky. Fingers of blue rippled their fringes playing a silent tune. Percussive pinks and crimsons exploded on to the star-studded stage. Whirls of purple and red shape-shifted in the heavens. An exotic sea creature, a wraith, an angel. The air crackled with enchantment. The celestial carnival had begun.

A small group of figures stood motionless on top of a rock, their faces raised in wonder as the drama unfolded above them. Time stood still as they watched, transfixed by the dancing, coloured lights. Around them, a strange, lunar landscape, visible only in silhouette.

Lizzie sensed for the first time the pulse of the universe, the rhythm of the natural world. Science could explain the spectacle, but not how it made her feel. Awe-struck, for sure, but more than that. A visceral connection with the natural world. Something she'd never felt before. Her faith in science had been shaken when she'd saved her city from a deadly storm. Some things were beyond the realm of human understanding. She knew that now.

As the last of the serpentine shapes slithered off into the ether, Dr Galloway threw his arms up in the air.

'Now that's what I call magic!' he said.

The spell broken, the students started to chatter animatedly amongst themselves.

'Wow! That was amazing!'

'Did you see those colours?'

'It was incredible!'

'Wait till I tell my little sister. She'll be sooo jealous!'

Lizzie was one of ten students to join their science teacher on a dark skies mission to see the aurora borealis. She'd read about the phenomenon and seen pictures but never dreamed she'd witness it for herself on the first night of their summer science trip to The Badlands.

Before they left their vantage point, Dr Galloway asked if there were any questions.

'I know the lights are caused by electrically charged particles from the sun entering the earth's atmosphere,' said Josh, Lizzie's science buddy, 'but why are they different colours?'

'Good question Josh,' said Dr Galloway. 'When electrons and protons enter the atmosphere, they hit gas atoms and molecules such as oxygen and nitrogen. The collision excites the atoms, causing them to give off light. The colour depends on which gas molecule is struck and its position in the atmosphere. Oxygen at sixty miles up gives off a yellowy green light. At two hundred miles or more it glows red. Nitrogen emits blue and purplish-red colours.'

There was a murmur of interest from the students but no more questions. Disappointed, Dr Galloway said: 'You're very lucky to have seen the Northern Lights you know.'

'Why's that then Sir?' piped up Sam Carruthers, a cheeky chap with long, blonde hair tied back in a ponytail.

Sam liked Dr Galloway because he always scolded students he caught teasing Sam about his hair.

'For one thing, you can only see them if you're close enough to the earth's magnetic pole. You need very clear skies with no clouds, and it has to be sufficiently dark.'

Some of the students started yawning and talking amongst themselves. Dr Galloway took the hint.

'Right. We better make our way back to the tents. You can ask more questions on the way. Switch on your torches and follow me!'

He strode down the hill in the direction of their camp. The students meandered after him across the undulating landscape.

'Josh, come here a minute,' said Lizzie. She was hanging back behind the group.

'What's up?' he said.

'Look over there.' She pointed to a dark shape on top of a mound in the distance.

'What is it?' he said.

'I don't know, but it's been there all the time we were watching the aurora. Whatever it is, I think it's been observing us.'

'There aren't any large wild animals this far from the mountains.'

'I know. Let's go and find out what it is.'

'Is that such a good idea?' said Josh. He remembered their escapade in Macimanito's Skyway the previous year. Poking their noses in someone else's business had landed them in a locked cell and nearly cost his family their lives.

'We'll be fine,' said Lizzie. 'We're not in the big, bad city now you know.'

Besides, there's something special about tonight and I don't want it to end, not just yet anyway.

They both started walking towards the silhouetted figure. Lizzie held her torch high, directed at the shadowy presence. About fifty metres away the beam picked out a flash of white. As they drew closer more features became visible.

'I think it's ... It can't be ... Kitchi!' Lizzie ran up to the figure and hugged him round the waist. The man took his one, good hand from the pocket of his long coat and patted her on the back.

She looked up into his damaged face, shrouded in long white hair. A lopsided smile broke through the raw, twisted flesh. She remembered how terrified she'd been the first time she saw his scars, before she got to know him. In the months after the great storm Kitchi had become a friend of her family. It started when Lizzie had insisted her mum invite him to dinner. She wanted to probe him about her dad's role as a geophysicist when he and Kitchi had worked together. Lizzie had only her mum's version of what her dad had been like. She wanted to know about Charles Chambers the scientist. The dinner invitation was followed by another and then another. Lizzie's grandpa had gradually warmed to the strange-looking man, once he felt sure Kitchi wasn't trying to take over his role as Lizzie's confidant. Her mum was quicker to accept Kitchi. Maybe she felt a First People's kinship with him. Maybe she sensed his strong moral compass. Whatever the reason, he soon became a frequent visitor to the Chambers' household and a firm friend.

'What a surprise. Why are you here?' said Lizzie.

'Did you enjoy tonight's display?' said Kitchi.

'Yes, it was amazing. I've never seen anything like it.'

'The Takoda, my people, *your* people Lizzie, believed that the dancing lights were the spirits of their forefathers celebrating life and creating a pathway for souls to travel to the next world. It is said that our ancestors dance in the heavens only when we are living properly and performing our ceremonies.'

'They must be pleased,' said Lizzie. 'Look at the show they gave us tonight!'

'On the contrary. The lights in the skies used to be much brighter, the colours more vivid. They are moving more slowly and last for a shorter time as each year passes. Our ancestors' displeasure is growing. They have brought sickness to our people living in the city and the nearby reserves.'

Another First People's myth or could there be some truth in it?

She used to dismiss her ancestors' stories as nonsense, borne out of superstition. Only when she learned of the magnetic anomaly under the city and its influence on storms, did she finally understand the legend of the monster beneath the streets.

'Why are you telling me this Kitchi?' she asked.

'You must help the Takoda.'

'But why me?' She instinctively raised her hand and squeezed the buffalo-bone talisman around her neck. It had belonged to her great-grandfather, a tribal warrior.

'Takoda blood runs in your veins. You were destined to save the land Macimanito stands on and you fulfilled that task. Now it is time for a greater challenge. You must find something sacred that has been lost. It will give our people renewed hope.

'The Badlands hold many hallowed places for the First People, some of which are deep underground, their location long since forgotten. According to legend, a sacred stone, formed by a fireball that streaked through the sky thousands of years ago, is hidden in one such place. It was revered and worshipped by all the tribes. For that reason, Christian missionaries in the nineteenth century tried to take it away and destroy it. A tribesman spirited it away and hid it in an underground chamber.

'The Takoda believe that if they find the sacred stone, their ancestors will look down on them favourably once more.'

'But where do I start looking?'

'Follow your instinct Lizzie. It will serve you well.

SCIENCE CAMP

Lizzie had trouble sleeping that night. Kitchi's parting words had stayed with her: 'Your great grandfather was gifted and a leader of our people. You share that gift and must put it to good use.'

What gift and why me? I want to be a scientist not some shaman in touch with the spirit world.

Still, part of her was looking forward to seeing where her instinct would lead her this time.

Kitchi had accompanied them back to their camp where twenty tepees dotted the rugged landscape like cone-shaped spaceship on the moon. Some were illuminated from within. The last image Lizzie remembered before finally dropping off to sleep was the sinister shadow play of featureless human forms behind canvas.

Dawn's rosy hue had long since given way to a brilliant blue when Josh poked his head inside her tent.

'Wakey, wakey lazy bones. You'll miss breakfast if you don't get up soon.'

'Uurgh ...' Lizzy rolled over on the wooden camp bed, her sleeping bag twisting round her. She was in no mood for his chirpiness. She scanned the tepee with one eye half open and realised the two other girls sharing her tent were gone.

'Josh Stapleton!' Dr Galloway's voice boomed out from the dining tent. 'Kindly remove yourself from one of the girls' tepees and come and help me serve breakfast.'

'Okey dokey Sir. I'll be there in a minute!'

'Now, Stapleton,' came the reply.

'Come on Lizzie. Today's the day we go to the dinosaur museum. You were so excited about it yesterday,' said Josh.

'Whaaat?' Lizzie said, still half asleep. Suddenly the words 'dinosaur' and 'museum' hit home.

'Cripes!'

She tried to spring up. Encased in a cocoon of nylon and polyester, she hopped once, twice, and then flopped sideways on to the ground like a giant caterpillar.

'Ppfff...' spluttered Josh.

'OK. The show's over,' said Lizzie. She'd managed to wriggle her arms free and lever herself into a sitting position. 'Go! And keep some toast for me!'

Josh wandered off towards the smell of cooking bacon.

Lizzie disentangled herself and hastily dressed in shorts, t-shirt and sandals. The sun was already warming up the tent. Soaring summer temperatures were forecast for the entire week. As per camp regulations she slapped sun block on her spindly arms and legs and tucked her wayward black curls into a Science Park baseball cap. She polished her dark-rimmed glasses on a discarded sock and hooked them over her ears.

'Right. Breakfast.' she said, heading out.

Twenty-four boys, twelve girls and six teachers from Macimanito High School were attending the camp. Lizzie had not intended to come. She'd been awarded a year-long pass to The Badlands Science Park by the city's mayor, in recognition of her courage the previous autumn. She and her family could go any time for free. But Grandpa had been poorly, and her mum needed to stay and care for him. She suggested Lizzie join the school trip.

Breakfast was a communal affair. Long tables and benches had been assembled in a large rectangular tent. The sounds of sizzling bacon and sputtering eggs were barely audible above the chatter of excited thirteen-year-olds.

Lizzie collected her plate of food and sat down beside Josh.

KNOCK! KNOCK! KNOCK!

Dr Galloway banged the table and rose to his feet.

'Silence please! After breakfast we're going to the world-famous Royal Clarkson Museum of Palaeontology, a two kilometre walk from our camp. We'll spend all day there, exploring the museum, watching films about the work of the palaeontologists and undertaking science projects. Our museum guides, who will also be accompanying us on the walk this morning, are three placement students from the South American Natural History Museum. Feel free to ask them as many questions as you like about anything dinosaur- or fossil-related. That's all! We'll meet at the camp entrance in half an hour.

***

Maria, Felipe and Sebastian introduced themselves to the gathered students and teachers. They gave their names and the local fossil sites where each of them was working. Maria, a tall, elegant-looking young woman with long, auburn hair coiled on top of her head, led the way across the hilly, barren terrain.

Lizzie knew the landscape would be different from anything she'd ever seen before. Naturally curious, she'd heaved 'A Geological History of North America' off the sagging shelf in her bedroom the night before they'd left and opened the section entitled 'The Badlands'.

She learned that early French trappers and fur traders had given the region its name because of the inhospitable territory. Over thousands of years, the area's weak sedimentary rock had been etched by the weather and eroded by water as the ice sheets retreated leaving deep narrow, winding gullies and fantastical rock formations.

Now, as they walked through the landscape, Lizzie could sense the ancient forces at work, grinding and shaping the land. They passed through gullies where the steep rocks on either side appeared to have been petrified in mid-flow. Deep incisions divided the swollen flow patterns like giant claw marks. Escarpments bulged with bulbous stone warts and swollen pillars supporting rocky mantels.

'Notice the layers of rock in the hills,' said Felipe with a Spanish accent. He pointed to the red, white and grey stripes visible in the mounds all around them. Bearded, with short, dark hair sprouting from beneath a wide-brimmed hat, he was not much taller than some of the pupils.

'Can anyone tell me the names of some of them?'

'Sedimentary,' said Sam.

'That's right. And what does that mean?' said Sebastian. He was at least six inches taller than Felipe, clean-shaven with a thick mop of black hair.

'It means it's made up of deposits of different types of rock.'

'Like sandstone,' said Lizzie.

'And coal,' Josh joined in.

'You know a lot. I am impressed,' said Felipe. 'And where there is coal, you often find what?'

Stony silence.

'Dinosaur fossils, of course!' he said, throwing his palms out wide.

'Uurgh ... yeah.' The students realised they'd already forgotten some of the geology notes Dr Galloway had given them on the bus to camp.

The time soon passed as the students took in the unusual rock formations, chatting to their guides and among themselves. When it was clear the pupils had run out of questions, Felipe and Sebastian started talking to each other in Spanish. The discussion soon became heated. They spoke rapidly, raising their voices and waving their hands around.

'I wonder what they're talking about?' Lizzie said to Josh.

'Beats me. I don't know any Spanish, do you?'

'Nope.'

'I do.' The high-pitched voice came from the blond ponytail in front of them. 'We had a Mexican au pair when I was little.'

Sam turned to Lizzie and Josh.

'OK clever-clogs. What are they talking about?' said Lizzie.

'Well, my Spanish isn't great but I did pick up the words "*No le diga al director*", which means "don't tell the boss", and "*feta*" which is the same in English - "feta", as in feta cheese.'

'Mmm ... sounds like a lot of baloney to me,' said Lizzie.

'No. I definitely heard the word feta,' said Sam.

'Why would they want to keep something about cheese secret from the head of the museum?'

Lizzie instinctively felt something was wrong but barely had time to digest Sam's words when the museum loomed into view. Its low-rise layers of pink sandstone and glass mimicked the sedimentary rocks surrounding them.

'RAAAAA!'

A giant, green Tyrannosaurus Rex guarded the entrance.

THE ROYAL CLARKSON MUSEUM

'OK. Gather round,' said Maria in broken English.

Three huge carnivorous dinosaurs gazed down on them. Mouths open, revealing jaws filled with razor-sharp teeth. Their muffled roars mingled with the sound of rustling vegetation and tweeting birds. The tableau thrilled Lizzie and the other students who chatted excitedly in the first gallery of the museum.

'We split you into three groups of twelve, said Maria. 'One group go with Felipe to watch film about geology of The Badlands and dinosaur fossil finds in this region.

Another go with Sebastian for behind the scenes tour. Final group comes with me to look round the museum. You will all get chance to do everything, don't worry.

'But first!' She raised her voice as everyone started shuffling in the direction of their favoured guide. 'Here is Dr Eli Smithson, the museum's curator, who would like to welcome you to The Royal Clarkson.'

Casually dressed in a checked shirt, jeans and trainers, a tall, athletic figure walked towards them from the direction of a small, glass office. A tousled thatch of grey hair topped a nut-brown face which was hewn with years of exposure to the sun on fossil hunting expeditions. Deep gullies lined his forehead and crevices cut into his cheeks and around his eyes. Rectangular wire spectacles framed periwinkle blue eyes that sparkled with pleasure as he approached the students.

Lizzie immediately warmed to the craggy-faced curator. His enthusiasm was infectious as he explained how the museum was named after geologist James Taylor Clarkson, who discovered a seventy-million-year-old dinosaur fossil skull in 1885 only a few miles from where the museum stood.

'In the great dinosaur rush of the early 1900s, droves of palaeontologists from all over the world came to The Badlands to search for the finest specimens to take back to their countries. This is still a hot bed of fossils and new discoveries are made here every year. More than twenty-five species have been uncovered so far.

'We are the only museum in North America dedicated to the science of palaeontology and we house the world's largest collection of dinosaur fossils. Scientists like Maria, Felipe and Sebastian,' Dr Smithson nodded at the three guides, 'come here every year to look for fossils and prepare them for research and display.'

A hand shot up from the group of students.

'A question! Yes, young man!'

'When we go fossil hunting tomorrow, if I find one, can I take it home to show my mum and dad?' asked Sam.

'Unfortunately, not. We are in an area protected by law where collecting is not permitted.'

Sam's face fell.

'But you will be palaeontologists for the day, which means that if you find a fossil, we want you to photograph it and make a note of any visible features. Try and mark its exact location on the map we give you. If it is loose on the surface, please bring it to the museum. If it is buried, bring us your photograph of the specimen and we can try and identify it together. You never know, you might find a completely new species of animal!'

Sam's face lit up once more.

'OK. Enjoy your day! I leave you in the capable hands of the three musketeers.' He looked from Maria to Felipe to Sebastian. They begrudgingly smiled at Dr Smithson's little joke.

'Let's go on the museum tour first,' Lizzie said to Josh. 'I can't wait to see all the dinosaur fossils.'

'Can I tag along?' said Sam. He looked over his glasses at them with a serious expression on his face.

'Of course you can, can't he?' said Josh, turning to his friend.

Lizzie hesitated. She liked having Josh all to herself. He was her science buddy after all. Sharing had never been her strong point, especially when it came to people. She remembered when her mum had persuaded her to ask a school friend over for a sleep-over. 'Make sure it's a girl!' she'd said. Lizzie didn't have any friends who were girls, but she'd invited Ali over anyway - they'd talked a couple of times at least. Lizzie's mum had made such a fuss of her.

Ali had lapped up the compliments and the cakes. Lizzie was furious. How dare her mother pay so much attention to someone else! It had taken a quiet word from her grandpa to explain to Lizzie that what she was feeling was jealousy. Her mother being nice to Ali didn't mean she loved Lizzie any less. Once in a while, it was good to share her mum with another person.

'Come on then,' Lizzie said to Sam. Josh looped an arm round Sam's shoulder. All three moved towards Maria. She was standing by a gigantic door to one side of the Albertosaurus display.

When her quota of twelve students had gathered round her, Maria said, 'Follow me and remember not to touch anything. I tell you about some of the exhibits and then you are free to wander around by yourselves. We meet back here in two hours.'

On their way out of the first gallery Lizzie stopped in front of a huge window cut into the wall. It gave a view of the fossil preparation lab. 'Ah yes,' said Maria. 'Let's look in here for a few minutes.'

The high-ceilinged room housed fifteen workstations. Steel-topped tables with sturdy legs. Over each hung a looping, concertinaed, black tube attached to a blue metal box with 'KZ Arm Airflow Corp.' printed on the side. Men and women wearing face masks, ear defenders, goggles and gloves leaned over fossil-bearing rocks on two of the tables. They were carefully drilling the specimens with hand-held tools or dusting with brushes. Sandbags supported the rocks. The light of a high-powered table lamp illuminated the fossils. Nearby tables were cluttered with electric drills, brushes of all sizes and other fossil preparation paraphernalia. Everything was covered in a film of rock dust. It clouded the air.

The students stood silently, watching the palaeontologists at work.

'What are they doing Miss?' asked Sam.

'When the fossils are brought into the lab,' she said, 'they are usually encased in the rock in which they were found. Here we gently remove the loose sediment and stabilise the fossil with a sort of glue and hardener, so it doesn't fall apart. Many have cracks in them.'

'And what's that big green door for?' said Lizzie, pointing to a twenty-foot high roller door at one end of the room.

'That is for when we find something really big, like the complete skeleton of a Camarasaurus. We bring it right into the lab on the back of a truck. We use the heavy-duty crane up there,' she said, pointing to a yellow metal beam in the ceiling with a giant hook attached, 'to lift it off and place it on pallets on the floor.'

As she finished speaking a cluster of faces appeared in the glass of the double doors opposite, inside the lab.

'Ah, there is the other group with Sebastian,' said Maria.

The two groups of students waved and pulled faces at each other through the glass.

Then Felipe appeared and said something into his colleague's ear. Sebastian ushered his students out the door and followed Felipe into a recessed area of the room housing shelves of boxes, plastic bottles and trays. After a few minutes of intense discussion, they looked over at Maria and gestured urgently for her to join them.

'Ah, OK,' she said. 'I leave you now to explore by yourselves. No running and no touching remember. I catch up with you later.' She walked quickly back in the direction they'd come from.

The students visibly relaxed with no adult in charge. Most of them raced off deeper into the museum. Lizzie, Josh and Sam stayed by the window. They saw Maria enter the lab and walk over to her two colleagues. They huddled together. Felipe seemed to be doing most of the talking. Maria looked alternately exasperated and worried, holding her face in both hands or gesturing angrily at Felipe. Sebastian was frowning. He held one arm tightly across his body and held his chin in the other hand.

'I wonder what that's all about?' said Lizzie. 'They're arguing again.'

'Don't suppose you can lip-read Spanish?' she said to Sam hopefully.

'Eh no,' he replied.

'There's definitely something going on with those three,' Lizzie said, 'and if you were right about what you heard Sam, it sounds suspicious.'

Lizzie sensed they were up to no good. She made a mental note to keep an eye on the three guides. Not right now though. They had the whole museum to look round!

'Come on - let's explore!' she said.

On Lizzie's lead the three of them turned and wandered towards the next gallery.

A waist-height barricade made of plywood separated off part of the adjoining room where a new dinosaur fossil skeleton was being assembled. Solid-looking bone segments articulated the massive, curved neck of the beast, continuing along its spine and gargantuan tail. Supported on giant leg bones, the skeleton was almost complete. Only its skull and a few rib bones were missing. A pair of tall, metal step ladders stood alongside the creature. Welding equipment, ropes and various tools littered the floor.

As they walked past the incomplete display, a glass cabinet in the far corner of the gallery caught Lizzie's attention.

'Hey, look at that!' she said, wandering over.

Six, dark brown objects lay in a bed of brown earth inside the display case. Their surfaces pimpled like reptile skin and criss-crossed with deep crevices. Alongside the cabinet, hanging from the wall, the photograph of a tall man in a trilby hat. A stiff white collar, smart trousers and shiny black shoes peeked out from beneath a luxurious ankle-length fur coat. Standing in a rocky landscape, he gazed down at something in his cupped hands. It looked like one of the objects in the glass case.

Josh read the legend out loud: "Barnum Brown, the American palaeontologist, finds the world's first Tyrannosaurus eggs in The Badlands."

'Wow! These must be T-Rex eggs! Sam beamed.

'I wonder if any more have been found,' mused Josh. 'What do you think Lizzie?' Josh knew his friend had been swatting up on dinosaurs before the science camp.

Lizzie wasn't listening. Her mind was elsewhere. A thought was tugging at the back of her brain. Something Sam had said. She tried to hold on to it, but it was as slippery as a salamander. Her train of thought lost, her eyes aimlessly levelled with the photo of the famous palaeontologist. She noted the incongruity of his outfit in the barren landscape, the deeply tanned face gazing in admiration at his find. Then, without warning, the man in the photograph looked up and smiled.

EGGS

'Ah. You've spotted one of our rarest finds I see.'

Dr Eli Smithson materialised out of nowhere. Lizzie, still stunned by what she'd seen, remained silent.

'These little beauties,' he said, 'are the first and only Tyrannosaurus Rex eggs ever found in the world.'

'Cor! Where were they found?' asked Sam.

'Only a few kilometres from here. So, when you go fossil-hunting tomorrow I want you to keep your eyes open. There may be some more out there.'

'Yay! We're going on an egg hunt!'

'The T-Rex was one of the biggest dinosaurs that ever lived, wasn't he?' said Josh.

'Yes. We know that much but otherwise he remains a bit of a mystery,' said Dr Smithson. We still don't know much about his lifestyle and biology. If only we could find a fossilised embryo ...' Dr Smithson sighed wistfully,' ... now that really would be something. The babies probably had feathers you know.'

'Feathers?' said Sam.

'Oh yes. Palaeontologists believe that dinosaurs like T-Rex were forerunners to modern-day birds, so there is every likelihood the young ones at least would have had a covering of feathers.

'Anyway, I must get along. Enjoy!' He strode off.

Lizzie noticed movement above. Strange shadows danced on canvas sails suspended from the ceiling. They reminded her of the human forms that had spooked her first night's sleep at camp. She shivered.

In the next gallery the gigantic skeleton of an ancient alligator hung vertically from the wall, still embedded in its stony sarcophagus. Its head was raised, its jaws open in its final death throes.

'Look,' said Josh, 'It says on the sign that teenagers found this dinosaur fossil. Wouldn't it be great if we found something really important too, like Dr Smithson said?'

'Aren't you forgetting something?' said Lizzie. 'I'm supposed to be searching for the Takoda's sacred stone.'

'Sacred stone?' asked Sam.

'Do I tell him?' she said to Josh.

Lizzie didn't wait for a reply.

'OK Sam. You mustn't tell anyone, especially not the other students or Dr Galloway.'

'No problem. My lips are sealed.' He pulled an imaginary zip across his mouth. 'So ... What is it? What is it?' The tension was too much for him to bear.

Lizzie explained what Kitchi had told her. This made Sam even more excited.

'Yes!' he clapped his hands with glee. 'A real treasure hunt. Where do we start looking?'

'Well, that's just it,' chipped in Josh. 'All we have to go on is that it's some sort of rock from outer space and that it's probably buried underground.'

Sam's face fell.

'Is that it? No clues?'

'No, that's it,' said Lizzie. 'Kitchi told me to follow my instinct, so that's what I shall do.'

'Who's Kitchi anyway?' said Sam.

'I am,' said a rasping voice behind them. All three jumped and turned round. Sam visibly shrank behind Josh at the sight of Kitchi's scarred face.

'Do you trust this boy?' Kitchi asked Lizzie.

She hadn't really thought about it. Her mouth had got the better of her again. Perhaps she shouldn't have told him.

'Yes. He's our friend.'

'I am their friend,' Sam echoed in a tiny voice.

'There is something you need to know Lizzie,' Kitchi said. 'It may help in your search. The First People have known about the dinosaur fossils in The Badlands for thousands of years, long before the Americans and Europeans started digging them up. Our people believed large water monsters roamed the earth long before man. The monsters fought with giant thunderbirds and those that died in battle turned to stone. Our people chose to leave these fossilised beasts in the earth. It is believed that the sacred stone lies among these ancient creatures.'

'Well that narrows down the field a bit!' said Sam sarcastically, his courage restored.

Kitchi fired him a withering look.

'I won't be far away. If you need me, my old friend Dr Galloway will know where to find me.'

They watched him exit the gallery.

'How does he know Dr Galloway?' Sam asked.

'It's a long story and we haven't got time for it now,' said Lizzie. 'Let's go and find the others.'

They walked up through a tunnel of multi-coloured lights denoting different geological eras into an eerie glass-bottomed room of primeval sea creatures. As they moved through a connecting corridor a row of macabre fossilised reptile heads glared at them from a glass wall cabinet. The eyeless sockets in their bony masks seemed to follow them out of the room. The three friends finally caught sight of their group in the dinosaur hall. They passed through an arched chamber housing a flattened Triassic giant.

'Urr..' Said Sam. 'It looks like an enormous bit of road-kill.'

'It's actually a dolphin-like marine reptile called Ichthyosaur Shonisaurus Sikanniensis,' said Lizzie, reading the narrative on the wall.

'Easy for you to say,' snorted Josh.

They headed into the main exhibition hall, a vast, high-ceilinged room housing dozens of reconstructed dinosaur skeletons.

'Wow! Look at that!' said Sam. His eyes opened wider as he scanned the hall. 'So many dinosaurs in one room!'

Partitions painted with imagined landscapes from the Cretaceous period separated tableaux of giant herbivorous dinosaurs grazing or submitting to a carnivorous cousin in mid-fight. Enormous sea and airborne dinosaurs were displayed swimming or flying, their huge jaws wide open ready to snap at the nearest prey.

Standing in front of a Lambeosaurus, the other students were listening to Maria, who had re-joined her charges. Lizzie, Josh and Sam sidled up to the back of the group.

'... distinctive crests on top of their heads, believed to be used for making noises and recognition in social settings.

'OK. You have enough of museum?' said Maria. 'Now we go behind the scenes. Follow me.'

The students traipsed after her through a door hidden in the wall behind one of the partitions. They emerged into a corridor with long, white walls interrupted by a series of dark blue doors. Each one was labelled. They passed the 'Casting Laboratory', 'Research Laboratories', and 'Prepared Collections' before arriving at the preparation lab which they'd seen earlier through the viewing window. They all peered through the door at the palaeontologists hard at work.

On one wall Josh noticed a hand-written list of current dig sites. He spotted Maria, Felipe and Sebastian among the names of palaeontologists assigned to each one.

'Where will we be looking for fossils tomorrow?' he said.

'None of those,' Maria replied, gesturing to the list. 'Those are official digs designated by the Royal Clarkson. You will be going to the fossil beds in Horseshoe Canyon, not far from camp.'

'How do you decide where to dig?' asked Lizzie.

'We look at geological maps for places where the age of the rock is right for finding dinosaur fossils and where it is exposed. We scan the area with binoculars and do a lot of walking, examining the ground as we go. Of course, not all fossils are found on top of the ground. Sometimes you have to dig a little deeper to find what you are looking for. There is a lot of suerte, how you say ...?'

'Luck?' said Sam.

Maria looked quizzically at him.

'Yes, luck. There is quite a lot of luck involved.'

'And that's exactly what we'll be needing tomorrow,' Lizzie whispered in Josh's ear, as they followed Maria out of the hall and into the theatre.

FOSSIL HUNT

The trek to Horseshoe Canyon took the school group through Red Buck, the only town in the region. As they walked along Main Street past a row of dusty shops, Lizzie noticed an advertising hoarding in the distance, by the side of the road leading out of town. As they came closer, she was able to read what it said:

The Badlands Passion Play

July 8-24

Travel back 2000 years to events that changed the course of history in Red Buck's magnificent natural amphitheatre!

'What's a passion play?' she asked Dr Galloway.

'It's a theatrical version of events leading up to the death of Jesus Christ. The Badlands Passion Play is world-renowned and has won lots of awards. You'll be pleased to know we all have tickets to go and see it on the final Friday of camp.'

'Uurgh ... Sirrrrr!'

The thought of spending hours watching a religious play held little appeal for the students.

'Now, now, don't be like that,' said Dr Galloway. 'It's as much about experiencing open-air theatre in a spectacular landscape as anything else.'

'What has passion got to do with it?' chipped in Sam. 'My dad says I have a passion for insects. What did Jesus have a passion for?'

'Ah well, this is a different sort of passion. In this context it means suffering and is derived from the Greek word *pascho*.'

'Can we skip going if we're not Christian?' asked Lizzie. Neither her mum nor grandpa had ever taken her to church or mentioned religion, so she suspected she wasn't a Christian.

'No, I'm afraid not. I've cleared it with all your parents. We're all going. Besides, there won't be anyone around to supervise you that evening. Everyone who lives round here takes part in the play one way or another. The town will be quite deserted.'

Maria, Felipe and Sebastian, who were guiding the group, exchanged glances at this news.

Leaving the town, the group left the road and made their way along dirt tracks for another forty-five minutes. By the time they arrived at the canyon and descended to the bottom of the coulee, the sun had burnt off the early morning mist. The air shimmered with the first heat of the day.

'OK, here we are!' said Felipe. 'Time to go fossil hunting!'

'Yay!' Everyone cheered.

The evening before, all the students had been given a tool kit to carry in their backpacks. It included a small shovel, a trowel, brushes and a sieve.

'If you find something, remember to treat it with the utmost gentleness,' said Felipe. 'Fossils are very fragile. Brush away any loose debris. If it is embedded in stone, take a photograph and mark on your map where you found it. If it is loose and not too heavy, you can put it in your bag and bring it back to the museum. Happy hunting!'

There was a buzz of excited chatter as the students scattered in groups of two and three to explore the canyon. Dr Galloway and the other teachers wandered among them, their enthusiasm rubbing off on the students.

Before long, ecstatic cries rang out from the walls of the gully.

'Found one!'

'Me too! Look at the size of this!'

'I've found an egg! I've found an egg!' said Lizzie.

The three South American guides, who'd been sitting together on a rock cluster, rushed over to look at Lizzie's find.

They burst out laughing when they saw what it was. Lizzie's look of surprised delight turned to a scowl.

'What's so funny?' she said.

'This is no egg carino,' said Sebastian, smiling. 'This is, how you say, caca.'

'He means poop,' said Sam, not smiling.

'It's coprolite, fossilised poop,' said Sebastian.

'Oh.'

Lizzie felt embarrassed, disappointed and angry all at the same time.

'Well they look like the eggs in the museum,' she said.

'Perhaps a leetle bit,' said Sebastian, placing a consoling hand on Lizzie's shoulder.

She shrugged it off.

Hmph! Smarmy post-grads. They certainly came running when they thought I'd found eggs, didn't they? I wonder why they're so interested in fossilised eggs?

Lizzie was grateful that neither Josh nor Sam had laughed at her mistake. She had heard a few titters from some of the other students nearby. Her friends knew better than to make fun of her. She took herself very seriously.

As time passed and more and more students started finding fossils, Josh said: 'You know I reckon most of these fossils have been planted here. We're finding them too easily.'

'What do you mean?' asked Lizzie.

'Well, I seem to remember when I was reading up about The Badlands camp it said something about students being given an authentic fossil hunting experience.'

'Meaning?' said Lizzie.

'Meaning that the museum has put fossils in the ground here so that we all have a chance of finding one. So, none of us is disappointed. I wouldn't be surprised if these weren't even real fossils.'

'That's outrageous,' said Lizzie. 'We need to go on a real dinosaur hunting trip, especially if we're to discover where the sacred stone is hidden. There's no point trying to explore existing sites being surveyed by the museum's palaeontologists. They won't let us anywhere near them.'

'There's always the old coal mine,' said Sam.

'You mean the one on the other side of town?'

'Dr Galloway said it had been boarded up since the 1980s when it closed down,' said Lizzie.

'So... when has something like that ever stopped you, Lizzie Chambers?' said Josh.

'You're right! It's definitely worth a look. Remember what Felipe said. Where there's coal there's sometimes ...'

'Dinosaur fossils!' said Sam.

'That's right! We just need to think of a way to sneak away from the main group without being noticed.'

Sam took off his hat and shoved it to the bottom of his backpack. Then he poured some water from his drinks bottle into his hand and rubbed it through his hair.

'Aargh!! Aargh!!' he cried, crouching down and clutching his head.

'Sam. What's wrong?' said Lizzie.

'Sir, sir! There's something wrong with Sam,' said Josh.

Dr Galloway galloped over and gently lifted Sam up into a standing position.

'What's the matter Sam?' he said, looking into his face.

'I think I'm getting heat stroke Sir. My head hurts and I feel really sick.'

'Where's your hat?'

'I forgot it Sir. Must have left it in my tent.'

'His head is soaked with sweat,' said Dr Galloway. Another teacher had come to help. 'Call the camp medic and get him to come and take Sam back to the first aid tent.'

The teacher did as he was asked and within fifteen minutes a four-wheel-drive vehicle appeared. The driver cautiously navigated the steep slope of the canyon.

'In you get lad,' said Dr Galloway as the vehicle pulled up. Sam looked urgently at Lizzie and Josh, who only then realised what he was up to.

'Can we go with him?' they asked quickly. 'We're his best friends.'

'Oh, alright then,' said Dr Galloway. 'While Sam's resting you two can read up about the dinosaur fossil finds in North and South America so you can give a talk on them tomorrow.'

'Righto Sir!' They hopped into the car beside Sam.

On the way back, Sam kept up the pretence of suffering from heat stroke, moaning every now and then and holding his head in his hands.

'Nice one!' whispered Josh in his ear.

Sam turned his head and smiled.

Lizzie maintained a serious look on her face in case the medic was watching in his rear-view mirror.

When they arrived back at camp, all three followed the medic into the first aid tent. Sam was asked to lie down on a makeshift bed. An electric fan was pointed in his direction and switched on. He was given a glass of water to sip at intervals and a couple of painkillers to swallow.

'I'll be sitting outside if you need anything,' said the medic.

As soon as he was out of the way, Sam sat up and the three friends started whispering urgently.

'The coal mine is a ten-minute walk from here,' said Josh.

'How are we going to get past the medic?' asked Sam.

'All of these tents have two entrances,' said Lizzie. 'Come on, let's scarper before he realises we're gone. We've got some exploring to do!'

THE GHOST

As soon as they were clear of the camp, Lizzie and her friends moved quickly. They stayed close to the hills, avoiding the town so they wouldn't be seen. The dark speck in the distance gradually grew bigger until they could make out the rickety-looking structure supporting the external mine works. On top of the wooden framework sat a huge, rectangular building which extended all the way into the side of a nearby hill.

'Wow! It's enormous!' said Sam. 'What is it?'

'It's called a tipple,' said Lizzie. She remembered a science through the ages project on mining she'd completed in the winter. 'Inside is a mechanism for carrying out all the coal mined inside the hill and loading it into railroad carts ready to be taken away. Let's go inside and have a look!'

They climbed up a set of steep steps on one side of the building and entered the gloomy interior. The mid-afternoon sun struggled to penetrate the tiny windows running along both sides of the elongated structure.

Inside, a canvas conveyor belt at shoulder-height stretched in both directions as far as the eye could see. It was supported on metal rollers, caked in decades-old grease. Following Lizzie's lead, the friends negotiated the narrow walkway alongside the transporter. Strips of wood had been fixed across the upward sloping floor as footholds. At the end they came to a set of huge, metal cogs. At this point the building made a ninety degree turn and continued its upward trajectory into the side of the hill.

'This must be how the coal was transferred from one conveyor belt to the next,' said Lizzie.' Look. The walkway ends here. We need to find a way to get inside the mine itself.'

They exited down another external staircase and scrambled up to where the wooden building met the hillside.

'There's a separate entrance over there,' said Lizzie. She motioned towards a vertical hole cut into the rock nearby. It was boarded up.

She went over and started pulling at the planks with all her might.

'Well don't just stand there. Give me a hand,' she said.

Sam retrieved a fossil hammer from his backpack and tried to lever off the lower boards.

'I don't think this is a good idea,' cautioned Josh. 'We're probably trespassing, and there's no guarantee it's safe.'

'Uurgh ... Aargh ...' Lizzie struggled on regardless.

'Lizzie ... Are you listening to me?' said Josh.

'Oh, come on Josh. Nobody's going to mind us trespassing. We're only kids and we're not going to damage anything. As to staying safe, I reckon if the tunnels haven't collapsed yet, they're not likely to do so any time soon.'

Josh didn't agree with his friend's logic but decided there was no harm in having a quick look.

'Oh, alright then. Let me do that. I'm stronger than you.'

'Oh no you're not.'

'Oh yes I am.' Josh heaved off one of the planks. Then another. And another.

'Humph ...' Lizzie had to admit he might be right.

At least I'm stronger than Sam. He hasn't managed to budge a single piece of wood either.

When a person-sized hole had been made in the boarding, Lizzie was the first to clamber through. 'Torches at the ready!' she said. 'It's going to be dark down there.'

They entered a tunnel created by a series of arches. Heavy wooden vertical struts supported horizontal beams. The deeper they descended into the mine, the cooler the air became. A dank, earthy smell invaded their nostrils.

'I'm scared,' said Sam. 'I feel like I'm in a tomb and we're going to be buried alive.'

'Stop being so melodramatic,' snapped Lizzie. She didn't mean to be unkind, but Sam had asked to tag along with her and Josh. If he wanted to stay friends with them, he needed to be braver.

'I'll tell you what Sam,' said Josh. 'Why don't you stay in the middle of us two. Will that make you feel safer? It'll be like a Sam sandwich. What do you say?'

Sam chuckled at the thought of it. 'O...OK,' he replied. 'I suppose that might work.'

They stopped and Josh and Sam swapped places.

Eventually they arrived at a wider, more open area. Lizzie searched the ground and picked something up. It was a tin cup, covered in dirt.

'This must have been where the miners took a break,' she said. 'There's nothing much here. Let's keep going.'

Deeper and deeper into the hillside they went. Suddenly, a faint glow appeared up ahead. 'Do you see that?' said Lizzie, leaning to one side so the others could see past her.

'See what?'

'That light?'

'I can't see any light,' said Josh. 'You must be seeing things.'

Why can't they see what I'm seeing?

'It's an optical illusion,' piped up Sam.

'Oh, you two, honestly,' she said. 'What's wrong with your eyes? There's certainly nothing wrong with mine.' She took off her glasses and cleaned them on her shirt, just in case.

The glow didn't go away. As the three friends walked towards it, Lizzie could finally make out its source. An old-fashioned miner's lamp, held high in the hands of ...

She stopped abruptly at the entrance to a chamber. Her knees started to tremble. She reached up to her neck and clutched the arrowhead talisman for comfort. The apparition stood quite still, looking at her. Thoughts sparked through her mind.

This makes no sense. Don't panic! Don't panic! Who is it? How can I see him? Am I going mad? Need to run! Fright or flight? Flight!

Turning, she found her path blocked by Sam and Josh. They'd both been taken by surprise when she stopped and had stumbled forward into each other. She faced them, too afraid to speak, her eyes wide with alarm. Her mouth opened but no words came.

Out of my way! Escape! Escape!

Her face was a deathly grey. She froze.

'What's wrong, Lizzie?' said Josh.

Silence.

She steeled herself and slowly turned around.

Please go away. Please be gone.

The glow remained, as did the creature holding it. Knowing that her friends were behind her, she felt her courage return. She looked the spectre up and down. Its edges were blurry, its substance wavering and insubstantial like a mirage. It seemed familiar. The hat, the shoes, the fur coat ... it was Barnum Brown, the palaeontologist in the photograph at the museum!

As if reading her mind, the phantom smiled and gestured with its one free hand to a spot on the wall of the cavern. Its eyes followed, taking Lizzie's gaze with them. Then, without warning, it disappeared into the thin air of the mine.

Lizzie clasped her hands to her chest. She could feel her heart racing so hard she thought it would pop out of her rib cage. Relief gradually washed over her.

'Lizzie ... Lizzie ...' Sam and Josh tried to get through to her but she seemed lost in a trance.

'You look ghastly,' said Josh.

Ghastly or ghostly?

She'd read the various scientific explanations for so-called ghosts and wondered which one she'd just experienced. Whatever it was, it was very scary. It really did look like Barnum Brown. Of course, there may have been another explanation, but she didn't care to dwell on that. She was a scientist after all. Still, if the famous palaeontologist was trying to tell her something, what was it?

'Yes... yes... I'm sorry. Something really weird just happened,' she said.

'What? What?' said Sam.

'Oh, never mind. I'll tell you later.' Regaining her composure, Lizzie walked into the cavern and stooped down to take a closer look at the place the apparition had pointed at.

'I think I've found something.'

DISCOVERY

'We need a rota,' said Maria. 'The absence of one of us during the night will not be noticed but more than one… it is too risky. Particularly coming back in the early morning. We were almost spotted the other day.'

Maria, Felipe and Sebastian were sitting round the kitchen table of their lodgings in the town of Red Buck. The students' fossil hunt was over, and everyone was having lunch before the start of the afternoon's activities.

'Maria's right,' said Felipe, 'but we don't have much time. If we are to extract our *precioso descubrimiento*, our precious find, by the end of the week we each need to work four or five hours every night.'

'We have already made much progress,' said Sebastian, 'But the most difficult part is still to come. We need to drill the rock they are encased in so that we can lift them out. That is noisy work.'

'We are deep underground. No-one will hear us,' said Felipe.

'The trickiest part will be bringing them out of the cave,' said Maria. 'That will require all of us working together and we will have to park the truck near the entrance to the mine. Hopefully everyone will be otherwise occupied at The Passion Play when we make our move.'

Maria thinks of everything, thought Felipe. He had found the entrance to the cavern on a fossil scouting trip shortly after their arrival in The Badlands. Secreted in a hillside, away from the main mineworks, it must have been used as an alternative escape route for miners in the event of a collapse. Curious, he'd spent hours exploring the tunnels until he was confident he wouldn't get lost. Eventually he came to a chamber where a strange rock formation had caught his attention. Using his tools, he had brushed and scraped away at the surface until a cluster of domes appeared. Bringing his lamp closer he realised he had found a nest of fossilised dinosaur eggs. One was cracked all the way round. Carefully easing his trowel round the fissure, he gently prised off one half of the egg. '*Dios mío*!' He had jumped for joy. What a find!

On the way back from the mine Felipe had already decided not to tell Dr Eli Smithson about his discovery.

I will take them back to The South American Natural History Museum, he told himself. I will be a hero! If these are T-Rex eggs they will be our museum's first. I cannot let such a find stay here in North America. As to his other find ... well, that would be his little secret and his alone.

Felipe realised he needed Maria and Sebastian's help to extract the eggs, so he had told them about his discovery. Their initial excitement had turned to concern, however, when he told them he had no intention of telling the Royal Clarkson's curator.

'But he is our friend and mentor,' said Sebastian. 'We cannot do this to him.'

Felipe disliked Dr Smithson, for no other reason than he had charmed Maria from the moment he'd set eyes on her. They were always flirting with each other. This irritated Felipe who hoped to wheedle his way into Maria's affections himself.

'It is also illegal,' said Maria. 'We could be jailed in an American prison if we are caught trying to take fossils out of the country.'

'But think about what it will mean for *our* country and *our* museum,' Felipe said, 'not to mention our careers. We may be banned from North America if they find out but so what? We are South Americans and will be welcomed with open arms when they see our discovery.'

Eventually he'd won his colleagues over. Maria had agreed to get involved on condition she organised everything. She didn't trust the other two not to mess things up. Sebastian was less keen but was tempted by the promise of a fast-track promotion once he returned home. His father was the curator of their museum and would be impressed with their find.

Both Maria and Sebastian were aware that Felipe was an *inconformista*, a maverick, who liked to do things his own way. He also had a short temper and was quick to jump to conclusions. These traits, they assumed, stemmed from his childhood. He'd lived in the servant's quarters of a rich family home in Buenos Aires where his mother worked as a maid. The master of the house had finally taken pity on the boy, who was always hanging round his mother, and paid for his education. Rather than being grateful, however, Felipe had grown to resent the charity bestowed upon him. He had turned his back on the family and chosen a career they had positively discouraged. He wanted to show them he could make a success of whatever he chose to do.

In the weeks before the arrival of the school party, Maria, Felipe and Sebastian had spent their days working separately at the Royal Clarkson's official dig sites and their nights together, underground, carefully excavating their secret hoard.

'The students are an annoying distraction,' said Felipe, who had been making a list of the equipment he needed to take into the chamber that night. 'How I hate children! That silly little boy doesn't wear his hat and boom! He gets heatstroke.'

'Yes, but if it hadn't been for that *niño tonto*, that foolish child, we wouldn't have known that the medic has his own four-wheel drive vehicle,' said Maria. 'This is good to know. The trucks used to take us to the dig sites every day are too big, too noticeable to transport the fossils and us out of here and back to South America. A jeep, meanwhile ...'

'Good thinking,' said Felipe.

'There's something else we need to discuss,' said Maria. 'I may be wrong, but I think that boy can understand Spanish.'

'Little blondie, the ponytail boy?' said Sebastian.

'Yes.'

'No way!' said Felipe.

'It's possible,' said Sebastian. 'We need to be more careful what we say around him and his friends.'

'The girl with him strikes me as being a smart cookie, as well,' said Maria. 'She seemed to take a lot of interest in us when we were talking in the preparation lab.'

'As long as the students are confined to camp, the public areas of the museum and their own fossil-hunting patches we should be OK. Agreed?' said Felipe.

'Agreed,' said Maria and Sebastian together.

'If their curiosity gets the better of them and they stray too close to our dig site we'll deal with them as necessary.'

TYRANNOSAURUS REX

'What is it?' asked Josh. He peered over Lizzie's shoulder. She was crouching down by the wall of the chamber. Sam knelt down on her other side to take a look.

'There's something sticking out,' she said. Brushing away the loose earth with her hand, she saw a dark tip protruding from the wall's surface. It had a shiny brown surface. 'Can you fish my chisel and hammer out of my backpack,' she asked, afraid to take her eyes off whatever it was in case it, too, vanished.

'Here they are,' said Sam, handing her the tools.

She gently tapped around the object, loosening more earth until it was three-quarters exposed. Gripping the point between her thumb and fore finger she gave it a sharp tug. She wasn't expecting it to come free so when it did suddenly, she fell backwards on to the floor of the chamber, her legs sticking up in the air.

'Pfff...' Josh and Sam sniggered.

Lizzie felt silly. Her first instinct was to cover up her embarrassment by getting angry with her friends. But she knew they didn't mean any harm.

Sitting up, she extended her hand to show them what she'd extracted from the wall. The curved object was about the size of Lizzie's hand.

'It's a tooth!' said Sam.

'Look how big it is! It must be a carnivorous dinosaur tooth,' said Josh. 'Wow! That's amazing. Wait until we tell Dr Smithson.'

'I think you're right,' said Lizzie. She felt along its inside edge. 'It's not jagged on one side, though, and the tip is quite blunt. I thought carnivores needed teeth that could grip and tear meat.'

'All except one carnivore,' said Josh, his eyes opening wide with excitement. 'T-Rex! You've found the tooth of a Tyrannosaurus Rex! How lucky is that?'

Mmm ... It wasn't luck at all. More like a long-dead palaeontologist trying to give me a clue to something, but what and why? Barnum Brown's name will forever be associated with the eggs of the great dinosaur. Maybe he was trying to tell me where to find more.

'Hey,' said Sam, 'do you think there are any other teeth around?' He started searching the wall and floor of the chamber with his flashlight.

'I bet there are,' said Josh. 'Where there's teeth, there's usually a skull and where there's a skull, a whole skeleton.'

And maybe even some eggs? Lizzie wondered. She put the dinosaur tooth in her pocket and caressed it with the palm of her hand. She wondered if it would be a talisman like the buffalo-tooth that hung round her neck.

'Come on, let's keep looking,' said Josh. 'I think we're on to something.'

On high alert for any more fossil sightings, the three friends searched every inch of the chamber. They uncovered a couple more teeth in the wall, both of which were firmly embedded in rock.

'I wonder where the rest of the skeleton is?' said Sam.

60

Making their way out of the tunnel along a narrow passageway Lizzie, at the head of the group, stopped abruptly after a few hundred yards and took a step back.

'Whoa! Looks like we've come to end of this particular tunnel,' she said.

'How do you mean?' asked Josh.

'Look,' said Lizzie, 'but be careful, there's a steep drop.'

She stood to one side so that Josh and Sam could see what she was looking at.

A cavernous space opened out in front of them illuminated by their torchlight. About fifty feet below in the floor of the cave, water shimmered.

'The tunnel must have collapsed,' said Josh, 'or maybe there was an explosion.'

'There may have been a cave here all the time and the miners never knew about it.'

'Never mind how it got here,' said Lizzie, 'look what's down there.'

Her two friends shone their flashlights downwards.

'It's an underground lake,' said Sam.

'No - off to one side,' said Lizzie.

'Bones!' said Josh.

'Yay!' shouted Sam. 'Yay ... yay ...yay.' His voice bounced around the cave.

'We've got to find a way to get down there and take a closer look,' said Lizzie.

'We'll need a rope and something to secure it to the tunnel floor,' said Josh.

'Maybe we should tell Dr Smithson first,' suggested Sam. He wasn't keen on heights and didn't fancy clambering down a steep rock face with only a rope to stop him falling.

'What, and have those snooty post-graduates ban us from the site before we've had a chance to see what's down there?' said Lizzie. 'No way!'

'I agree,' said Josh. 'This is our discovery, and we should explore it ourselves first.'

'Hold on a second,' said Lizzie, peering down into the cavern. 'Do you see those knobbly rocks over there? Are those ... they look like ...' She straightened up and looked at her two friends. 'I think there are some eggs down there. Do you realise what this means? We may have stumbled on the only other find of fossilised T-Rex eggs in the whole world!' She started jumping up and down in the air. 'Yes!' 'Yes ... yes ...yes,' came back the echo.

'Crikey,' said Sam, adjusting his torch so that it sent a narrow beam of intense light on to the spot Lizzie had been scrutinising a moment ago. 'I think she might be right.'

'We've got no time to lose then,' said Josh. 'Let's go and get those ropes.'

Threading their way back through the tunnels in the direction they had come, the three friends could smell the fresh air infiltrating the dampness as they approached the mine entrance. They stepped through, roughly replacing the boards, and headed back in the direction of their camp.

In the late afternoon sun, their three figures cast long shadows as they skirted the line of hillocks dotting the barren landscape. As they neared the museum, they noticed someone coming towards them.

Felipe had decided to check on the entrance to the cavern and try and devise a better means of covering it so that no-one else would stumble on it.

'Ah, my friends!' he said. 'Where have you been? Your teachers they worry about little blondie here.' Felipe ruffled Sam's hair, making him squirm.

'Oh, we just went for a walk. We thought it might do Sam some good, now the sun's less fierce. The painkillers seem to have done the trick,' said Lizzie.

'That is good, that is good. You go walk you say? Why your hands so dirty then? Have you been scrabbling up rocks or something, eh?'

'No ... nothing like that,' said Josh, trying to sound casual but failing miserably.

'The mineworks. They are dangerous you know. Closed for a long time now. Very unsafe. You mustn't go there.'

'We won't,' said Lizzie, smiling broadly and dragging her two friends off. 'We must be getting along. We're very hungry and I'm sure it must be almost dinnertime.'

'Yes, indeed. Off you go then.' Felipe's smile turned to a scowl behind their departing backs. Pesky children, he thought. I wonder what they've been up to. If they scupper my plans, I'll ... I'll ... He smashed his fist against the vertical rock face.

THE CURSE

'Listen up everyone,' said Dr Galloway, clapping his hands.

The after-dinner chatter quietened down.

'While Felipe and Maria light the fire pit, ready for this evening's little surprise....' There was an excited murmur from the assembled students. '... Lizzie and Josh are going to give a brief talk about the different dinosaur fossil finds in North and South America.'

Rats, thought Lizzie. She'd hoped their science teacher wouldn't remember. How were they going to bluff their way through this? She looked at Josh, who looked at Sam.

'Can I join in too?' Sam asked Dr Galloway.

'Well of course, if you feel up to it.'

Sam gave his two friends a reassuring nod and together they walked to the head of the long dining table. Sebastian fetched some plastic bottle crates for them to stand on.

'Ahem.' Sam cleared his throat. 'It is impossible to say for sure which dinosaurs roamed South America and which North America. There are too many gaps in the records of fossil findings.'

'These holes in our knowledge can span several million years,' said Josh.

'When dinosaurs first appeared all of the world's countries were joined together,' continued Sam. 'Over the millions of years when dinosaurs existed, some continents moved closer together. This influenced where different dinosaurs were found.'

'They may also have been affected by the climate in different parts of the world,' added Lizzie. She and Josh both realised what Sam was trying to do. He was being as vague as possible. Giving reasons why they couldn't talk about the different fossils found in North and South America.

'So,' said Lizzie. 'Our research shows that it is simply not possible to identify the differences between dinosaur fossil finds in North and South America.'

The three friends were about to step down from their makeshift podiums when Sebastian said: 'There is one dinosaur we have never found in South America of course.'

'Oh ... is there?' said Lizzie. Trust one of the post-grads to show them up, she thought.

'T-Rex of course!'

Felipe, who was heaving logs near the fire pit, stopped what he was doing. He threw a withering look in Sebastian's direction.

'We had Giganotosaurus, who was taller and faster than Tyrannosaurus Rex, but he was roaming South America thirty million years before T-Rex appeared. He was also carnivorous and about seven tons in weight.'

'Fascinating, fascinating,' said Dr Galloway. 'Thank you for that nugget of information Sebastian. Looks like someone did their homework.' He frowned at Lizzie, Josh and Sam.

'Now. Everyone gather round the fire pit. We have a special treat for you tonight. Felipe is going to tell you a tale from The Badlands.'

'Sir!' some of the students protested. They thought they were far too old for bedtime stories.

'Now, it's not any old story. It's the story of The Lost Lemon Mine.'

Not convinced, they reluctantly took their seats on the logs round the fire. Dr Galloway and the other teachers handed round cups of hot chocolate.

Felipe started pacing round the fire pit, his face taking on a demonic glow in the reflected heat of the flames.

'Many, many years ago there was a man called Bill Lemon and his friend Blackjack who found rich diggings of oro, gold, east of the Rocky Mountains,' he began.

'They carried their hoard on horseback to The Badlands where they made camp, much like we have here. Late that night they argued terribly about what to do with their riches. They had been drinking rotgut, a mixture of alcohol, wine, red peppers and ginger. Lemon waited until his friend slept and then wham!' Felipe sliced the air with his outstretched hand. 'He smashed his wood-chopping axe into Blackjack's head, splitting it like a melon.'

'Uurgh!'

Despite their initial reservations, the students were enthralled by Felipe's animated storytelling.

'The next morning, he was horrified at the sight of what he had done. Lemon pánico, how you say? panicked. He stayed with the body of his friend two days and two nights, undecided what to do. Then he buried the body and hid the gold before heading back to the nearest town.

'Lemon's terrible act of violence prayed on his mind. His reason left him. When he tried to find his gold the following year, he could not remember where he had put it. The more he tried to find it the further his reason slipped away from him.

'Over the years many people searched for the hidden gold. One was struck down with a mysterious sickness. Another was burned in a fire that consumed his house. Another died suddenly during the night. It was as if there was a curse on whoever searched for Lemon's blood-stained gold. To this day, Lemon's gold has never been found. It is rumoured to be buried somewhere near here, among the fossil grounds.'

There was stunned silence.

'Sir? Can we go searching for the gold?' said one of the students.

'Yes Sir. Can we?'

'Please Sir!'

Before Dr Galloway could answer, Maria said, 'Like all good tales, this one has a moral. Do you know what that means?'

'A lesson Miss,' said Sam.

'That's right. The moral of this story is that you shouldn't go searching for someone else's riches, especially if blood was shed in obtaining them. If you do, your life will be cursed forever!'

'I think she made that up,' said Lizzie quietly to Josh.

'Me too,' he said.

Lizzie wondered why they had chosen that particular night to tell them this story. Could it have anything to do with them meeting Felipe on the way back from the mine?

By the time the students left the fire side and dispersed to their tents, night had fallen. The inky sky twinkled with stars, a spattering of atomised silver on a blue-black canvas.

Lizzie felt compelled to stop and gaze at the spectacle of the night sky.

'This is my favourite place on earth,' said a familiar voice.

She turned. It was Kitchi. He smiled.

'There's another version of the story you heard tonight,' he said. 'Would you like to hear it?'

They walked over to a rocky outcrop and sat side by side on a slab of limestone as he began his story.

'The prospector Lemon had a wife, a First People's widow who had a son aged eleven. The three of them, with Lemon's partner, set out with their cache of gold to make the journey back to town. They stopped for the night in a cabin where Lemon and his partner slept. This is where he hid the gold. Lemon's wife and her son slept in shelters outside. In the evening when Lemon went out to fetch wood, his partner followed him and killed him. He told Lemon's wife her husband was still out in the bushes, gathering firewood. She suspected the worst and told her son to hide. She found Lemon's body and kept an overnight vigil, swearing to avenge him. The other man ransacked the cabin looking for the gold. In the morning Lemon's wife built a fire and served the man breakfast. While he sat with his back to her she raised an axe and split open his head. She buried Lemon with his gold and placed a curse on the place so that no white man could take the gold that belonged to her husband. Only when his bones had crumbled to dust would a person of First People's blood find the gold.'

'So Lemon wasn't the murderer after all?' asked Lizzie.

'And the gold rush was much further west than The Badlands, at the foot of the Rocky Mountains. Lemon would have no reason to venture this far,' said Kitchi. 'But who knows which story is closest to the truth. One thing this version of the story does tell us is the First People's attitude to gold. Lemon's wife could have taken the hoard and become a wealthy woman, but she left it with him in the ground. That's because the gold taken out of the earth by white men often came from land sacred to the First People, near burial grounds. The land was more precious to them than gold.'

'Like their sacred stone?' said Lizzie.

'Yes, like their sacred stone,' said Kitchi. 'How is the search going for our ancestors' treasure?'

Lizzie hesitated.

Should I tell him about Barnum Brown appearing to me in the coal mine? What if it had nothing to do with the sacred stone. I'll look such a fool.

'It's going OK. I think I may have a lead. It's early days though.'

BARNUM BROWN

Lizzie spent the night wrestling with her thoughts and trying to calm her restless limbs. Her nerves were jangling like wind chimes in the breeze. She had been in The Badlands two days now and was no closer to finding the Takoda's sacred stone. Or was she? She went over in her mind everything that had happened so far.

The post-graduate students were hiding something from the museum curator but what and why? The nineteenth century palaeontologist Barnum Brown seemed to be trying to tell her something. It was a bit freaky, him smiling at her from that photo in the museum and then 'appearing' in the mine. Maybe that was the gift Kitchi had been referring to when he compared her to her great-grandfather. Maybe she could see spirits. What was Barnum Brown trying to tell her though? Was it about the T-Rex skeleton and eggs in the coal mine? He was the first person to discover T-Rex eggs after all. But why would he want her to make the discovery? Were all these things interconnected? If so, how? More importantly, how were they going to lead her to the sacred stone?

When she awoke the following morning after a few hours' sleep, she was more determined than ever to make sense of everything. But first her school group were going to visit an actual dig to watch real palaeontologists at work. After that the students were free to explore the museum and the surrounding area. That would be her chance to go back to the coal mine with Josh and Sam.

They were trucked to a dig site near Horsethief Canyon. Felipe was one of the palaeontologists excavating the fossil skeleton of a large, herbivorous dinosaur. The students were allowed to wander around the site, staying outside the roped-off areas so they didn't stand on any delicate fossils.

'Where's Felipe?' said Lizzie to Josh and Sam. 'I thought he was supposed to be here.'

No sooner had she spoken than a jeep appeared over the hill. When it reached the site, Felipe jumped out. He exchanged a few words with the medic before he drove off. Felipe yawned and sluggishly made his way down into the canyon.

'Good afternoon Mr Fernandez!' said the leader of the dig. 'So glad you could join us!'

'Sorry I'm late boss. Slept in. My alarm. It is broken I think.'

'Well don't let it happen again. We have a schedule to follow. This little beauty needs to be out of the ground and into the museum before winter.'

Felipe dropped his bag of tools. He sat down opposite another palaeontologist who was brushing earth off what looked like a huge thigh bone.

'I wonder what's up with him?' whispered Lizzie. 'Look at the dark rings under his eyes. He looks barely awake.'

The three friends sat down by an area where four people were meticulously uncovering the long spinal cord and tail of the dinosaur.

'This would be a good place to pick up the rope and securing hooks we need for the mine,' said Josh. 'There are coils of rope under the specimen bench. Look.' He jerked his head backwards.

'I'll get them,' said Sam. He was eager to please his new friends.

He casually walked over to the trestle table that had been set up on the canyon floor and took off his backpack. Bending down, he pretended to search the ground. When he was sure no-one was looking, he quickly stuffed a coil of rope into his bag, then some metal loops. He ran back to his friends.

'Got them!' he whispered.

***

'Hello my old friend. Come and have a cup of tea,' said Dr Galloway. 'I'm just composing the questions for the end of camp quiz.'

Kitchi sat down opposite his former school classmate at one end of the long dining table.

'What brings you to The Badlands?'

'I need to ask a favour Maurice,' said Kitchi.

'It's not like you to come asking for favours from me. You were always the resourceful one at school. Do you remember the time you got hold of some potassium permanganate and were going to do that experim ...'?

'Never mind that. This is important.'

'OK, OK. I'm listening. What can I do for you?'

'Lizzie Chambers.'

'What about her?'

'I know the family. I worked with her father Charles on the geophysical surveys of Macimanito. Lizzie's involvement in saving the city from the hurricane last year was no accident.'

'But I thought the university had devised some kind of storm deterrent.'

'That's the story the Mayor wants the public to believe. The truth is Lizzie saved the city.'

'But how? I don't understand ...'

'It doesn't matter how. All you need to know is that the gift bestowed on Lizzie by her First People's ancestry is in the ascendancy. She is becoming more and more in tune with her instincts. The Takoda people, my tribe and hers, need her to use her powers to find something for them. Something that has been lost for more than a hundred years.'

'Why are you telling me this Kitchi?'

'This sacred object. It is here in The Badlands. Give her some leeway Maurice. Let her search. Do not restrict her to the confines of the camp programme. Let her use her intuition to find it.'

'Well, that's all very well but I have a duty of care ...'

'Give her this little bit of freedom Maurice. What's the worst that can happen?'

'Well... anything,' he blustered.

'Not on my watch. I'm staying in Red Buck. I will keep an eye on her. She won't see me, but I will see her. Have no fear.'

'I'll think about it,' Dr Galloway conceded. 'Now stay with me a while and help me think of some more questions for the students.'

The two old friends sat in companionable silence, flicking through books.

'I must include a question about Barnum Brown, the 19th century palaeontologist,' said Dr Galloway. 'He was quite a character, you know. Apparently, he ingratiated himself with some native tribesmen. I imagine he had to - he was plundering their land after all! There's even a rumour they showed him the location of those T-Rex eggs he's so famous for discovering.'

Now why would they do that? thought Kitchi. It didn't make sense. Maurice must be mistaken. Then he remembered seeing the strange look on Lizzie's face that day in the museum. She'd been standing by the glass case of eggs with the photograph of Barnum Brown on the wall next to it. Lizzie had told him what had happened. Perhaps there was some truth in the story about how the fur-coated palaeontologist found those eggs.

THE COAL MINE

'It was just a silly story,' said Lizzie.

'But what if Lemon's gold is in the mine and we'll be cursed!'

'Oh, for goodness sake Sam, Felipe made it up to try and scare us, that's all. Now let's get on with it.'

'I'll go down first,' volunteered Josh.

'No. Me first,' said Lizzie. 'I've secured the rope to that metal loop with a bowline knot. I want you to keep an eye on it Josh, just in case the rock gives way. Sam can come down after me and then you last.'

That afternoon the three friends had told Dr Galloway they were going to search for fossils a little off the beaten track.

'Ok, but stick together and stay safe,' he'd said, giving Lizzie a stern look.

Making their way back to the mine as quickly and discreetly as they could, they retraced their steps to find the cave entrance.

'I'm at the bottom ... bottom ... bottom,' echoed Lizzie's voice. 'You next Sam ... Sam ...Sam.'

'I'm not sure ... I don't think I can ....'

'Take a deep breath and don't look down,' said Josh. 'You can do it.'

Sam cautiously sat on the edge, took the rope in both hands and turned round. His eyes met Josh's as he lowered himself down. Josh gave him a reassuring smile as he began his descent.

'Well done Sam,' encouraged Lizzie from below. 'Now ease yourself down the rope.'

At the bottom Sam was triumphant. 'I did it, I did it, I did it!'

'I knew you would,' said Lizzie. In fact, she thought he'd chicken out. Whereas Lizzie and Josh knew each other's weaknesses and strengths, Sam was an unknown quantity. She'd taken a risk bringing their new friend along on their little adventure. But she'd made her decision and would stick with it.

When all three of them were safely at the bottom of the cavern they spread out to have a look around, their torches lighting the way. Lizzie headed straight for the strange-shaped rocks she'd spotted the previous day.

'It looks as though someone's been here before us,' she said. 'There are chisel marks on the stone and a heap of rock dust, as if someone's been brushing away loose debris.'

Kneeling down, she felt a smooth, rounded indentation in one side of a fused set of oval-shaped rocks. *Something's missing. An egg perhaps? But egg clusters are usually excavated together and taken to the preparation lab in their stone cladding before being separated. Why would someone take just one away?*

'There's something at the bottom of the lake,' said Josh. He was peering through the glass-like body of water. It appeared turquoise in the light of his torch.

Sam, who had been collecting fossilised teeth, came and stood beside him.

'What is it?'

'It's difficult to make out. Can you see it? It's right at the bottom.'

'Don't just stand there. Get in and have a closer look.' said Lizzie.

What had he seen? Could it be the sacred stone? Is that why Barnum's ghost had led her to this place?

'What happens if there's something ... nasty down there?' said Sam.

'Such as?' Lizzie was getting irritated.

'I'll do it,' said Josh, starting to take off his clothes. He wasn't relishing the idea of getting wet or freezing to death, but he wanted to impress Lizzie.

Stripped down to his underpants he started to wade in, trying not to show how cold he felt. His skin exploded with goosebumps as his body reacted to the temperature. Then, without warning, he bent his knees and plunged headfirst under the water.

Sam and Lizzie watched as he dove down, lifted something off the bottom and rose to the surface, gripping it in his hand.

'It's massive,' gasped Josh. 'Give me a hand.'

Lizzie hid her disappointment. She didn't want to diminish Josh's achievement. It wasn't the sacred stone. Its shape was all wrong. She and Sam leaned forward and grasped either side of the gigantic fossil, lifting it out of the water and on to the cave floor. Josh got out and shook himself like a dog, spraying water everywhere.

'Wow!' said Sam. 'It's a jawbone.'

'It has to be part of a T-Rex skull,' said Lizzie. 'Look at those teeth! Which means ... these *are* T-Rex eggs! Wait until we tell Dr Smithson.'

All of a sudden, the sound of clapping filled the cavern. All three of them swivelled their heads round to locate the source of the sound. They peered into the gloom as the echoes bounced around the chamber walls.

'Well done, well done children!' They heard Felipe's voice coming from a dark corner of the cave. 'A great discovery! Sadly, you were not the ones to make it. I found this cavern some weeks ago and have been working on the excavation.'

'But this site isn't on the official Royal Clarkson list of dig sites,' protested Lizzie.

'Not yet, not yet. I wanted to be sure of what we had found here before alerting Eli. In fact, I was going to tell him this very day. Now run along children. I will take care of everything.'

'No, we will not run along,' said Lizzie. 'How do we know you got here first? It could have been anyone. Why should you claim this discovery as your own?'

She wasn't going to give in that easily.

'Come on Lizzie, let's go,' said Josh. He knew how impetuous Lizzie could be and didn't want them to get into trouble.

'No, I won't,' said Lizzie stubbornly. 'Not until we get some answers.'

Sam started sidling towards the wall of the cavern from which they'd descended. He didn't like the tone of Felipe's voice.

'Oh well, suit yourself, ninos tontos, dumb kids.' He vanished into the darkness.

'Where'd he go?' said Josh.

'I don't know but I've some bad news. The rope's gone,' said Sam.

'What!'

'We're trapped!' wailed Sam. 'Now what do we do?'

KEEPING THE SECRET

'They know about the cave? How can that be?' said Sebastian.

'I don't know but we have to get rid of them.'

Felipe had blocked the secret entrance to the mine with loose boulders and returned to the students' lodgings. The children were contained for the moment. He had planned to deal with them himself but thought better of it when he found Sebastian sitting at the table drinking coffee.

'Hey, wait a minute! Stealing fossils is one thing but I'm not harming *ninos*, children. I didn't sign up for anything like that.'

'Well sorry buddy, but you're already involved. Simply by knowing about it you're an accessory.'

Sebastian leaped from his seat with such violence the chair toppled on to the wooden floor. He thumped his fist on the table.

'No! I tell you. I have nothing to do with this. We stop this right now.' He glared at Felipe who was taken aback by his colleague's outburst.

'Well what do you suggest we do, eh? They could ruin everything for us! If they tell Eli, we are finished.'

'They're just kids. We have to give them a reason not to tell, at least until we go. It's only for a couple of days.'

Although Felipe had suspected Lizzie and her friends were exploring the mine, he didn't think they'd actually find the cavern. When he caught them there, he'd been so surprised his first instinct had been to frighten them into silence. Now he was glad he hadn't threatened them. He needed their co-operation. The success of his plan was paramount, but he remembered what it was like to be a child intimidated by older, more powerful people. It wasn't a good feeling. Pretending to be nice to them would make it easier to persuade them to keep their discovery a secret, at least for the time being. But what did he and Sebastian have to bargain with?

'I have an idea,' he said. 'At the end of camp, prizes are awarded for the most original science project, best fossil drawing et cetera et cetera. We must present our own award to the team that has shown most promise as future palaeontologists. We can tell the girl that she and her pals will win the prize for discovering the eggs. But they have to tell no-one until the last moment.'

'You think that will work?'

'The girl is the leader of their little band. We convince her and the other two will follow. She is luchadora, a feisty one, but she is proud. I think she will like the idea of being recognised for a major new fossil find.'

'Let's hope so. We must let Maria know what's happening when we see her.'

'Maria? No, let's keep it to ourselves for the time being. You know how she worries. We will tell her just before the prize-giving.'

***

'It's getting c..c..colder,' said Sam. 'And d..darker.'

'No, it's not,' snapped Lizzie. Staying calm was one of the eight rules she'd memorized from 'A Guide to

Responsible Caving' she'd read a few months ago and she wasn't going to let Sam start to panic. Showing her annoyance with him was more likely to make him anxious though and she immediately regretted speaking to him so sharply.

'Here, take my spare jacket,' she said in a conciliatory tone, pulling a windcheater out of her backpack and handing it to Sam. 'I've some spare batteries for your torch if it runs out. Don't worry, we'll get out of here somehow.'

'We need to find another exit. Felipe must have got in somehow,' said Josh.

'Try and feel for any air movement,' said Lizzie. 'That usually means there is a passageway that leads to the outside.'

Sam stuck close to her as she picked her way across the stony floor towards the cavern wall. Josh went in the opposite direction. Lizzie felt for the talisman round her neck, squeezing the T-Rex tooth in the same hand. Her flashlight lit up the ground at her feet. She saw further evidence of more extensive excavation. Judging by the shapes of the indentations left in the rocks a number of fossilised remains had already been removed from the cavern. That meant Felipe was probably lying, and he had found the site some time ago. He had no intention of telling Dr Smithson. Maria and Sebastian must know about it as well. What were they up to? she wondered. Finding T-Rex eggs was a big deal. Why wouldn't they want to be recognised for making such a discovery? Something wasn't right but she couldn't quite put her finger on it - that single egg-shaped hole; why had someone removed that particular egg first? It must have been something special, but what? ... No. Could it be? The thought suddenly struck her. Had Felipe found the sacred stone? Was that it? She mentally listed everything Kitchi had told her about the stone's whereabouts: deep underground - check; among the fossils - check; about the size of a large dinosaur egg (he hadn't actually said that but she imagined that was the case) - check. Felipe must have realised he'd found something extraordinary, dug it out and hidden it somewhere. But why would he take it? What did it mean to him?

'Josh, I think I know ...' she began to say when her friend's words rang out.

'Found it! There's the faintest of breezes coming from this corner of the cavern. Yes, there's a hole in the wall here. Come on, let's get out of here.'

The three of them followed Josh's lead, cautiously making their way along a tunnel that was only just wide enough and tall enough for them to fit inside. After what seemed like an eternity, they saw thin spears of light puncturing the darkness.

'That must be the entrance up ahead,' said Lizzie. 'It looks like there are stones piled in front of it.'

Before they had a chance to start dismantling the blockade, they heard someone on the other side starting to do the same. As more stones were removed and daylight started to flood in, Felipe's face appeared before them.

'Ah, I see you find your way out! Very good, very good. A little test you see - a bit of fun for you I think.'

'Fun!' said Lizzie. 'You deliberately left us in the cavern with no way of getting out!'

'Not at all, not at all. You see, I have come back for you. Here, I have brought water and some biscuits. I thought you might be hungry.'

Why is being so nice to us?

'Why did you take our rope and leave us in there?' she quizzed.

'A misunderstanding. You seemed so happy with your discovery I thought I leave you a little longer to familiarise yourselves with the site, you know, like proper fossil-hunters.

'On which note - I tell you in advance that all three of you will be winning the science camp special prize for the students who show the most promise as future palaeontologists. This is such a major find.'

'We know that but...'

'No buts. The prize is yours. I ask you only one thing. We make big splash with this at the end of camp. So, you must stay very quiet about it, how you say - keep mum, tight-lipped, tell no-one until just before the prize-giving. Then big surprise! What you say?'

'Well...' Lizzie did like the sound of being recognised for finding the second ever batch of T-Rex eggs in North America. Then she remembered about that peculiar, egg-shaped hole.

'Ok, we'll keep quiet on one condition.'

'What's that *chiquita*?'

'Tell us why one of the eggs has already been removed?'

Felipe hesitated.

'Removed? Well, it was quite loose in its stony surround and came out easily. The excavation of that one was simple. It is in safe place, don't worry.'

'Humph.' Lizzie was going to have to think of another way of finding out what he had actually taken away from the cavern.

'So, it is agreed? We have a deal?' said Felipe.

'Suppose so,' they all said in unison. Sam was simply relieved to see daylight and would have agreed to anything. Josh was curious to know what Lizzie had been getting at with her question but didn't want any trouble. He didn't trust Felipe. Lizzie was anything but happy. She wanted answers and was busy hatching a plan as to how she would get them.

NIGHT AT THE MUSEUM

'Bags I the stegosaurus,' shouted Sam as he ran into the Dinosaur Hall.

'Walk Carruthers! Walk!' said Dr Galloway. 'And keep your voice down. You'll wake the fossils.'

Sam found his favourite dinosaur skeleton and claimed his place in front of it. He lay out his sleeping bag on the floor and sat on top of it. Lizzie chose the Tyrannosaurus Rex in predatory pose. Josh took up position around the corner from his friend. By the time everyone had settled down the floor was festooned with a string of what looked like giant, multi-coloured teeth, each bulging with a wriggling body.

The excitement was palpable as the lights dimmed and Dr Galloway said, 'Night, night everyone! Breakfast is in the cafeteria at seven sharp. No wandering around. You don't want to find yourself being chased through the corridors by a dinosaur!'

It was the night the students had been looking forward to all week - a camp-in at the museum. All thirty-six pupils and six teachers were spending the night under the lofty roof of the palaeontology institute surrounded by the bony remains of ancient dinosaurs.

Lizzie, Josh and Sam had spent the day in the museum library. They'd told Dr Galloway they were researching the North American habitats of cretaceous dinosaurs. In fact, they'd been planning their next move. Lizzie was acutely aware that time was running out for her to find the sacred stone. There were only two days of science camp left. She couldn't let Kitchi and the Takoda people down. The humiliation would be unbearable. She decided to share her suspicions with her friends about Felipe finding the stone. Three heads were better than one to try and find where he'd hidden it.

'We have to search the rooms behind the preparation lab,' she said, 'and the house where Felipe and his friends are staying in Red Buck. They're the two most likely places where they could be hiding stuff.'

For their plan to work, they had to steal the keys that opened all those blue doors and find a way to break into the post-graduates' accommodation unnoticed.

'I'll do it,' said Sam. He was keen to prove himself to his new friends. 'I've seen a set of keys hanging in Dr Smithson's office near reception. I bet they open the doors to all the rooms. And I'll try and follow one of the postgrads and see if they leave a spare key anywhere.'

Spending a night in the museum proved the perfect opportunity to execute the first part of their plan. The three friends deliberately spaced themselves apart so they wouldn't arouse suspicion by leaving for the bathroom at the same time in the middle of the night. They had synchronised their watches and agreed to meet at midnight by the partition door leading into the main part of the institute.

As the other students and teachers drifted off to sleep, Lizzie, Josh and Sam stayed alert, counting down the hours until their rendezvous. Then, one by one they stealthily slipped out of their sleeping bags and made their way out of the dinosaur hall and into the room housing the flattened marine reptile. They crouched down together by the door in the wall.

'Did you get the keys?' whispered Lizzie.

'Yes,' said Sam. 'I had quite a job. Dr Smithson was glued to his seat in front of his computer most of the afternoon. I had to wait until he went for lunch and then he locked his office door behind him. I had to ask …'

'Ok, Ok,' she said impatiently. 'We don't need to hear the whole saga. Give them here.'

Lizzie took the bunch of keys and tried a few before she found the correct one. The partition door opened, and they stepped into the corridor, closing the door behind them.

Using their torches to light the way they came to the first door, marked 'Archive Room'. Lizzie unlocked it after a few failed attempts.

'It would be more efficient if we split up and each searched different rooms,' said Josh.

'Good idea. I'll take this one. Here are the keys.'

'Can I tag along with you,' Sam said to Josh. He was feeling nervous again. This place gave him the creeps.

'OK. Come on, let's go,' said Josh.

Lizzie was confronted with row upon row of steel shelves. They were packed with books, box files and tubes of rolled drawings. Every item was labelled with a sequence of numbers and letters which meant nothing to her. She almost turned round and left. How on earth was she going to search this place? Then she remembered her talisman. Instead of reaching for the bone buffalo tooth around her neck she instinctively felt for the T-Rex tooth in her pocket, smoothing its surface with her fingertips. As she did so, it became warm under her touch. She started to walk. A few moments later she stopped opposite a file marked 'BB 1860-1920 photos'. She took the box file off the shelf and sat down on the floor with it cradled in her lap. She opened the lid and started looking through its contents. There were lots of grainy, black and white photographs of what looked like dig sites. Groups of people excavating fossils in the Badlands landscape. She found the picture of Barnum Brown in his fur coat. It was probably the original of the print she had seen that first day on the wall by the T-Rex egg case. BB - it must stand for Barnum Brown. At the bottom of the pile of photos was another picture of the famous palaeontologist. This time a First People's tribesman was in the photo with him. Both were smiling broadly at the camera. They appeared to be shaking hands. No, the man dressed in a broad brimmed hat with a sort of rug thrown over his shoulders was handing something to Barnum Brown. Lizzie peered more closely at the photo. It appeared to be an egg. An egg! Hang on a minute. Her brain tried to compute this new information. Why would a tribesman be handing over an egg? Unless …

'Psst … psst …' Josh's shadowy figure appeared at the doorway.

'Whaaat?' she whispered.

'We've found something. Something important.'

Lizzie got up and put the file back on the shelf, her mind reeling from what she'd just discovered. Barnum Brown and the First People of the Badlands were connected somehow. Was that what his ghost was trying to tell her? But how were they linked?

'Come quickly,' said Josh, as she left the archives room.

'It's so exciting!' whispered Sam. 'You'll never believe what we've found.'

'Why don't you just tell me?' Lizzie didn't have the patience for playing guessing games.

'You'll see soon enough,' Josh said. He didn't care how irritated Lizzie became, he was going to enjoy the big reveal. He wanted to impress her with what he'd found.

He and Sam led her into the 'prepared collections' room which housed floor to ceiling cabinets of variously-sized drawers. Each was labelled with a dig site name, date and a brief list of contents. He stopped in front of one of the cabinets.

'As you can imagine, I didn't know where to begin,' he said, 'so I started looking for anything a little bit out of the ordinary.'

'Like labels that didn't look right, or muddy fingerprints or …'

'Exactly!' interrupted Josh.

'I noticed that the label on this drawer,' he said with a flourish, 'was hand-written, whereas the others were typed. And the floor in front of it was gritty underfoot.'

'So?' said Lizzie.

'I opened it of course. At first there seemed nothing unusual, until I realised the depth of the drawer from the outside didn't match the depth inside. When I lifted the fossils off the top layer in their foam cushion, dah! There was a second layer underneath. And in there, we discovered, this!'

Josh carefully scooped out an egg, which he cradled in his hands to show Lizzie.

'It's a fossilised egg.'

'It's in two halves. Lift off the top half,' he said.

Lizzie did as she was asked and let out a gasp. Nestled inside the egg was a perfectly preserved baby dinosaur.

'It's an embryo!' she said.

'And not any old embryo. It's a fossilised T-Rex embryo. The first ever to be discovered. Look, some of the soft tissue has been fossilised. You can make out the head and the tail.'

Wow! So, this must have been what Felipe had removed from the cavern site. Not the sacred stone after all. Her mind went back to the first conversation they'd overheard between their guides. Suddenly, she realised the mistake Sam had made in translation.

'It wasn't feta cheese you heard the students talking about Sam. It was foetus. They'd discovered a baby dinosaur!'

'Oh yeh!' Sam felt a little foolish. 'The two words are very similar in Spanish. It makes sense now.'

'I still don't understand why the post-grads are keeping this find a secret,' said Lizzie.

Josh took the egg from Lizzie and replaced it in its hiding place, next to the post-graduates' cache of eggs taken from the cavern. 'It is strange,' he agreed. 'This discovery is going to make news all over the world, so why haven't they told Dr Smithson about it?'

Lizzie wasn't listening. She was confused. She'd been so sure Barnum had led her to the secret dig site to find the sacred stone. Otherwise why lead her there? How could Barnum and the T-Rex eggs help her succeed in her mission?

SAM

The following morning after breakfast Sam told Lizzie and Josh he was going to stake out the post-grads house and find where they kept the spare key. There were still questions to be answered and searching their place might reveal new information.

When he still hadn't returned by lunch time, his friends decided to go and search for him.

'I just need to go back to my tent and pick up a few things before we go,' said Lizzie. 'Wait for me by the camp exit.'

When she entered the tepee there was an envelope on top of her sleeping bag. She opened it and read the note inside.

'They've got him!' she said, running towards Josh. 'It's not signed but it must be from Felipe or one of the other students. The spelling's all over the place. It says "Speak to Eli and you will not see your little friend again. Cover for his absence till the end of camp. Then we will let him go. Not before." He must have thought we'd tell Dr Smithson. Do you think he knows we found the embryo?'

'It's possible though I don't see how. Unless one of them saw us last night.'

'We've got to find Sam,' said Lizzie.

'Let's start at their house in town,' suggested Josh. 'They may have caught him trying to break in and locked him up inside.'

The two friends headed for the track behind the museum and set off in the direction of Red Buck. As they approached the end of the street where the students lived, they saw two of them leaving. Lizzie and Josh ducked behind a nearby dwelling.

'It's Sebastian and Felipe,' said Lizzie.

As they turned the corner out of sight, a shambling figure walked past from the opposite direction and went up the stairs into the house. It was Maria.

'What's wrong with her?' whispered Josh. 'She looks ill.'

Lizzie and Josh entered the lane running along the back of the row of houses, staying close to the fence. When they reached the students' dwelling, they silently lifted the latch on the back gate and crossed the yard at lightning speed, pausing for breath only when they had reached the back wall of the house. They heard a soft tapping.

'What's that noise?' said Josh.

'It's coming from ... Sam?'

Lizzie leaned sideways towards the direction of the sound and found herself looking at the blurry face of their friend framed in a filthy little window in the wall under the back stairs.

Sam was mouthing something through the glass but neither Lizzie nor Josh could make it out.

'He's in the basement,' said Josh. 'They've locked him in the basement.'

'He's waving something in his hand,' said Lizzie.

'It looks like a bit of paper with writing on it. He's pointing behind him. What's he trying to tell us?'

'I don't know but whatever it is, it looks urgent. We've got to find a way in,' said Lizzie.

They gave Sam a reassuring thumbs-up and sneaked round the side of the building.

'Give me a leg up so I can see in that window,' said Lizzie.

Josh cupped his hands for her to stand in and she cautiously levered herself up to the windowsill. She peered inside.

'Maria's in there. She seems to be sleeping on the sofa in the living room.'

'Where's the door to the basement?'

Lizzie scanned the room.

'I can't see it from here. We'll have to go in.'

'But what if Maria wakes up?' said Josh.

'There's no point thinking about what ifs now. We need to get Sam out of there,' she said, stepping down.

They crept up the outside stairs that led into the kitchen at the back. Lizzie looked inside the glass door to make sure Maria was still asleep and tried the door handle. Locked.

They heard an urgent tapping. Josh looked down to the basement window. Sam was tracing a rectangular shape with his fingers and pointing upwards.

'There must be a spare key somewhere,' said Josh. He bent down, lifted up a few plant pots, an old-fashioned milk urn and finally the cork door mat. 'Got it!' he said and handed the key to Lizzie.

Once inside, they could see the door that led down to the basement. Again, there was no key. As they stood there wondering what to do next, a sliver of white appeared under the door. It was the piece of paper Sam had been waving at them behind the window.

He'd written in what looked like charcoal:

Overheard them talking. Planning their escape during Passion Play. Going to South America with eggs. Get me out of here.

Lizzie put her finger to her lips and then gestured to Josh for them to leave. They silently left the house, closing and locking the back door behind them. Sam's face pleaded with them from the basement window.

'We'll come back and get you,' mouthed Lizzie. She wasn't sure if he'd understood her, but they had no time to lose.

'So that's their game,' said Lizzie. 'They want to steal the eggs and the embryo and take them back to their own museum.'

'But that's illegal,' said Josh.

'You bet it is. We need to tell Dr Smithson about this, and we need to tell him soon. But first, we've got to figure out how to rescue Sam.'

***

Maria had spent all night and most of that morning excavating in the cavern. When she finally awoke it was to the sound of distant snivelling. She sat up, stretching her long limbs upwards and outwards. What is that noise? she thought to herself.

Rising from the sofa she followed the sound into the kitchen and to the locked basement door. She pressed her ear to the wood. She tried the handle and heard a scuffling noise. Reaching on top of the door sill she fetched down the key and opened the door.

'Hola, is there anyone there?' she said into the darkness. No answer.

She switched on the light and started down the steps. At the bottom she scanned the space. It was filled with crates, an old bicycle, a washstand and other long-forgotten domestic paraphernalia. A movement in one corner caught her eye.

'What have we here?' she said. 'Little blondie. What are you doing here?'

Sam was huddled between two wooden boxes, his arms wrapped tightly around his knees that were drawn up against his chest. He looked dishevelled and very unhappy.

'You know very well,' he said quietly. 'Your friends locked me in here.'

'But no. There must be some misunderstanding. Why would they do that?' Maria tried to sound soothing. The boy was clearly distressed and babbling. What had Felipe done now, she thought, that idiot!

'Because ... because ... I don't know!' Sam started to cry.

'Oh, mi pequeno, come. Come with me.' She gently took Sam's arm and pulled him up on to his feet. 'Let's go upstairs and we can talk. I give you a drink.'

Sam climbed the stairs behind Maria.

'Sit down,' she said.' We will sort this out.'

Sam played along until Maria was busy in the kitchen pouring him a drink. When her back was turned, he seized the opportunity, opened the front door and ran as fast as he could back to camp.

Ah, a pity, thought Maria, when she realised he had gone. He might have been able to tell me what those two have been up to behind my back. Whatever it is, it won't derail our plans.

HATCHING A PLAN

Sebastian carefully loosened the rock and dirt around the final egg cluster with a small hammer and chisel and then brushed away the loose debris. When the fossils were clear of extraneous matter, he used a dropper to fill any visible cracks with preservative. He continued this process until the eggs were almost free of their rock bed and wrapped them in wet tissue paper before laying strips of plaster of Paris on top as a protective cast.

'Almost finished I see,' said Felipe, entering the cavern. 'I will cut the pedestal if you hold the eggs.'

This last manoeuvre freed the fossil completely. Together they carried the precious cluster through the passageway to the cave entrance. They carefully lifted it on to some old blankets on the back seat of the medic's jeep Felipe had borrowed earlier that evening.

'We won't have time to prepare this before tomorrow night,' said Sebastian.

'No, we will have to take it as it is. Just think, this time tomorrow we will be well on our way to South America with our precious haul. We will be famous Sebastian! Think of that!'

Sebastian mumbled something in response.

'What's that? Why aren't you excited man? This is a major discovery. Imagine how proud your father will be of you?'

That's just it, thought Sebastian. What was his father going to say when he realised where they had found the fossils and how they had snuck them over the border?

Together they went back to the cavern and collected their tools, making sure they left nothing behind.

'We need to block the entrance completely,' said Felipe. 'Come on, help me with these stones.'

Sebastian had been excavating at the site since before midnight and it was now four in the morning. He barely had the energy to keep his eyes open, let alone lug heavy rocks. Felipe was insistent they cover their tracks, however, and seal the cavern.

'What are we going to do with the boy?' asked Sebastian on the ride home.

'We feed him, we frighten him, we keep him subdued. When the time comes, we let him go.'

'And when will that be?'

'I'll be the judge of that.'

***

As soon as Sam reached camp he stumbled into his tepee and fell into a deep, exhausted sleep. He was woken by the call for breakfast the following morning. Instead of heading for the dining tent he went straight to Lizzie's. En route he bumped into Josh.

'Sam! How did you get out?' he asked. 'We cooked up a really neat plan to get you out today.'

'Maria let me out ...'

'Maria?' he interrupted. 'How come. She was in on it wasn't she?'

'I don't know if she is any more. We need to get Lizzie. I have loads to tell you.'

Their friend was already dressed when they reached her tent.

'Sam! How…'

'No time to explain Lizzie. We need to do something. Felipe and his pals are planning to leave tonight and take the T-Rex embryo and eggs with them! We have to stop them!'

'How do you know this?'

'When I was in the basement, I started to hear voices from above. It's an old-fashioned house with forced air heating that enters the rooms upstairs through open grates at floor level. The air is heated in the cellar and pumped up through ducts. When I put my ear close to the main pipe, I could hear them talking quite clearly.'

'But weren't they speaking in Spanish?' said Josh.

'That's the curious thing. They weren't. They were speaking in English.'

'Why would they do that?' asked Lizzie.' Unless … unless there was someone else there who didn't understand Spanish.'

'Someone must be helping them with their escape plan.'

'Anyway they're planning to collect the fossilised T-Rex eggs from the museum tonight at ten o'clock when everyone is at the Passion Play and then take the medic's jeep and head south for the border,' said Sam.

'We have to tell Dr Smithson,' said Lizzie. 'Now!'

'Wait a minute,' said Josh. 'Who is Dr Smithson likely to believe, some top-notch visiting post-graduates or a bunch of school students? Felipe and his crew will simply deny everything and say we're making it up.'

'But the evidence is there, among the prepared collections.'

'Do you honestly think they'll still be there. Felipe will have moved them by now. There are any number of other hiding places in the institute. Dr Smithson is hardly going to demand the place is searched on our say-so.'

'You're right,' said Lizzie. She realised she was being impulsive again instead of thinking things through. Josh's was the voice of reason and she needed to listen to him more.

'We must wait until they're about to leave and catch them red-handed,' she said.

'Then what will we do?' said Sam.

'You need to stay out of sight,' said Lizzie, ignoring his question. 'When they realise they have no leverage to keep us quiet about their discovery, there's no knowing what they might do.'

'Sam's right though. We need to think what they might do if we surprise them trying to flee,' said Josh.

'Mmm…' Lizzie's nose wrinkled up. She seemed to sniff the air. *Three of us against three of them. But they' re bigger and stronger than us. They may have weapons. The odds don't look good. What to do?*

'I know. We could ask Kitchi to help,' she said at last. 'He'll know what to do. Come on, let's have breakfast and then go find him.'

As they walked over to the dining tent Lizzie's thoughts started to drift. *What about the First People's sacred stone? Why did Barnum Brown want me to discover the eggs in the cavern if not to locate the stone?*

She felt the weight of responsibility in her heart as though the stone itself was lodged there. Foiling the post-graduates plan was a distraction she could do without, yet she felt compelled to go ahead with it. If she didn't find the stone perhaps it would find her.

THE ELDERS

'Welcome my friend. How goes it?'

The elderly tribesman's nut-brown face, weathered and creased, crinkled into a smile. The eyes were rheumy and very still.

'The news is not good, I'm afraid,' said Kitchi. 'Lizzie's quest to find the stone is proving difficult. She has little time left. You must prepare your people to be disappointed. She has the gift, there is no doubt about that, but perhaps she is too young to harness its energy.'

The two figures sat across from each other in Red Buck's only cafe. One upright, dressed in western clothes with long, white hair falling onto his shoulder, the other stooped with plaited, grey hair and rough-hewn trousers and jacket.

'That is a great pity. We were so sure. Perhaps she isn't the one the shaman spoke of.'

'What's that?' Kitchi thought the Takoda had told him everything when they approached him to ask Lizzie to find the stone. Clearly, he'd been mistaken.

'More than a hundred years ago, when the sacred stone went missing, it is said that a light-skinned man agreed to hide the stone in exchange for information.'

'What man was this?'

'The name was lost as the story passed from generation to generation, but they referred to him as the eccentric one. He was a fossil-hunter. A man of some status. He came here many times over the years looking for dinosaur bones. He found many, but the prize he really wanted always seemed to elude him.'

'What was that?'

'Eggs. Those of the mighty Tyrannosaurus Rex.'

'And did he find them?'

'He didn't, but our ancestors did. When he heard rumours that the local tribesmen knew the location of some fossilised eggs he asked to speak to their chieftain. A meeting was arranged. They didn't trust him at first. This man whose teams were disturbing the bones of ancient creatures. Many meetings followed. Trust between them grew. The shaman came up with a plan. They would tell the man where the eggs were located if he hid their sacred stone and tell not a soul about it … They shook on it.'

'And that was sufficient for the Takoda to trust this man with something so precious?'

'They made it clear that if he were to renege on his promise, they would hunt him and his family down and hang their scalps from poles at the entrance to their reservation. The settlers were very scared of the native people.'

'So where did he hide the stone?'

'If I knew that I wouldn't have asked you to send the girl out looking for it, now would I? The fossil-hunter asked the shaman where they wanted him to hide the stone and he said he didn't care as long as those scheming missionaries couldn't get their hands on it.

'Clerics had been sent over from Europe to try to convert us to Christianity. Sacred stones and other artefacts revered by our people were not considered helpful in this process. In the hands of the missionaries the stone would have been confiscated and then destroyed.'

'So was the stone ever meant to be found?'

'According to legend the fossil-hunter asked a similar question. He said, "how will it ever be found again?" and the shaman told him, "the one who is called buffalo will find it and return it to our people."'

'So, the story about the stone being hidden deep underground is untrue?'

'Who knows? The man never told the shaman where he hid it. He left these fossil grounds with the dinosaur eggs still in his possession. It was said they were later gifted to the Royal Clarkson museum by the man's ancestors, but I cannot confirm that story.'

Kitchi left the meeting deep in thought. The man his Takoda friend was talking about must be Barnum Brown. Lizzie was using her gift after all. That would explain why the famous palaeontologist kept appearing to her. Maybe she was closer to finding the sacred stone than she realised.

THE PASSION PLAY

Preparations for that evening's performance of the Passion Play were in full swing. A festive mood gripped Red Buck as Lizzie and Josh wandered into town the following afternoon in search of Kitchi. Townspeople dressed as disciples and Romans hurried off to the final dress rehearsal. Bunting had been strung across shop fronts and almost every window carried a poster advertising the play. As they approached J.P. Cartlett & Sons, the only grocer's in town, an aproned shop assistant inside turned the 'Open' sign behind the door to 'Closed'.

'Sorry' he mouthed through the glass. 'Early closing today.' He smiled.

They side-stepped the store entrance and knocked on the adjacent door leading to the rooms above. After a few moments it opened, and the giant frame of Kitchi filled the space.

'Ah Lizzie … and Josh,' he said. 'Come in, come in. No little friend today?'

'No. It's a long story.'

They followed him up a bare wooden staircase to a small living room cum kitchen. It was sparsely furnished with an old leather sofa and armchair at one end facing a fireplace. A table and four chairs occupied the other. An old-fashioned cooking range, wall-mounted cupboards and a sink unit completed the room. The place was devoid of any personal possessions.

'Sit down and I'll make us a cup of tea,' Kitchi said as they settled on to the settee.

'We need your help,' said Lizzie.

'With finding the sacred stone?'

'No, not that.' Lizzie's face fell. 'I don't think I'll ever find it.' Her voice reflected the disappointment she felt. 'Sometimes I feel I am so close, then the sensation dissipates and I lose it again. It's the strangest of feelings, like when a word is on the tip of your tongue, but your brain refuses to give it substance, to make it real.'

'So why have you come?'

Lizzie told him what Sam had overheard of the post-graduates' plan.

'We need your help to stop them.'

'Why don't you tell Dr Smithson, the museum's curator?'

'We don't think he'll believe us,' said Josh, 'and besides, there is a chance he is in on their plan.'

'I doubt that.'

'Well, Sam thinks one of the museum staff is in cahoots with them,' said Lizzie.

'Mmm … If your information is correct and we are to catch them red-handed, we will need to intercept them just before they leave. Here's what we'll do …'

***

A glorious sight greeted the students and teachers as they took their seats in the open-air amphitheatre. The sun, sinking into the horizon, gave a mysterious glow to the other-worldly mounds and layered hillocks of the Badlands. Roman centurions dressed in red robes and silver helmets stood guard either side of a huge wooden door in a stone fortress centre stage. People dressed in long tunics and cloth headdresses in earthy hues sat around talking. Others carried stone urns or ushered small children here and there.

'Cor, there must be hundreds of actors. Look at all the costumes,' said Sam.

'The entire town of Red Buck is involved one way or another,' said Dr Galloway. 'It's the big event of the year. There are only eight performances, and this is the first.'

Lizzie and Josh sat at the back near one end of a bench so they could slip away unseen. Sam sat next to them. He had kept out of sight all day, feigning another bout of heat stroke. He emerged at the last minute to join the other students as they walked to the Passion Play.

When everyone was seated and the trickle of late comers had ceased, the sound of trumpets filled the air, heralding the arrival of a procession led by two centurions.

As the students and other audience members sat transfixed by the unfolding spectacle, Lizzie leaned over to Josh.

'We'll leave about halfway through the second Act,' she whispered. 'When I give the nod, we go. Tell Sam.'

Josh did as he was asked. Sam looked over at Lizzie and gave her a thumbs-up. She didn't acknowledge him, however, as she was too preoccupied with the increasing warmth coming from her talismans, the buffalo tooth round her neck and the T-Rex tooth in her pocket. Her heart rate accelerated. She was filled with a sense of awe. Could the Passion Play be affecting her? What did it mean? She wondered if she was having some sort a religious experience. She'd read about someone who thought an angel had saved them when they had been swept out to sea by a current and nearly drowned. She didn't really believe it. If science couldn't explain such phenomena, they couldn't be true. Could they? She was beginning to have doubts. Maybe some things in this world happened for reasons beyond man's current understanding. She felt a sudden urge to leave.

Glancing at her watch, she realised it was time.

'Come on guys,' she said to Josh and Sam. 'Let's go.'

They quietly slipped out of their seats and headed for the exit. Down some stone stairs and across the car park they ran in the direction of the Royal Clarkson Museum. Kitchi was already at their agreed meeting place, lying flat on top of a small hill overlooking the museum.

'Look,' he said, nodding towards the museum. 'There's the jeep. I've already seen them load two crates of fossils.'

From their vantage point they could also see the front approach to the museum. As they watched, Maria walked around the end of the building and stopped beside a shadowy figure that had emerged from the front entrance.

'It's Dr Smithson!' whispered Lizzie. 'I knew he was in on it. The low-down, no good, palaeont ...'

'Let's not jump to conclusions,' said Kitchi. 'He's meeting with Maria but the other two don't seem to be aware of his presence.'

'Maybe he's going to stop them,' ventured Josh.

'Maria did let me out of their basement,' said Sam. 'She seems much nicer than Felipe and Sebastian.'

'I'm going to find out what's going on,' said Lizzie. Before Kitchi could stop her, she moved away. Crouching low to the ground, she ran round to the front of the museum, stopping once behind a low wall to make sure she couldn't be seen from the rear entrance.

'Dr Smithson. What a surprise!' she said, emerging from behind the giant model dinosaur in front of the museum.

'What the ...'

'I'll leave you to deal with this,' said Maria retreating into the building.

'What are you doing here?' he said to Lizzie in an urgent whisper. 'You're supposed to be at the Passion Play.'

'We know what you're up to and it's not right. We're going to stop the T-Rex eggs leaving here.'

'You and who's army?' he said. 'Besides, how do you know about the eggs? Oh, never mind. You have to get out of here.'

'My reinforcements are on the hill,' she said, gesturing towards Kitchi and the others.

'Well you and your buddies need to go now before you totally scupper my operation. Maria has told me everything and I have it all under control. Now go!'

Lizzie quickly realised her mistake. Her impulsiveness had nearly ruined everything. She rejoined the others and told them what was going on. Kitchi had his doubts that Dr Smithson alone could foil the post-graduates' plan, with or without the help of Maria.

'I have an idea,' he said. 'We'll enter the museum by the front so if Dr Smithson confronts them at the rear and they try to flee through the building we can stop them. For all we know they may have another vehicle waiting somewhere else.'

'Good idea!' they all agreed.

Stealthily they made their way towards the museum entrance. Dr Smithson had already disappeared. The staff door was unlocked. Inside they walked through the display of life-size carnivorous dinosaurs. Their silent menace followed the quartet as they passed the darkened preparation lab visible through the viewing window. Lizzie noticed a faint light behind the glass panel in one of the doors at the back of the lab. The post-graduates must still be decanting the eggs from their hiding places into the travel crates.

As Kitchi and the three friends entered the hall where the giant dinosaur skeleton was being assembled they heard shouting.

'*Andale! Andale! Arriba!Arriba!*'

Felipe came racing round the corner, closely followed by Sebastian. Dr Smithson was in hot pursuit.

'Stop them!' he cried.

Kitchi stood in the path of the fleeing men, his body slightly crouched, his scarred face turning puce as he braced himself for a fight.

Startled by the sight of such a large, scary-looking individual and with nowhere else to go, Sebastian and

Felipe jumped over the barrier into the dinosaur assembly area. They tried to double-back and return in the direction from which they'd come. In their haste Felipe accidentally bashed against the tall stepladders standing beside the incomplete skeleton.

'Look out!' cried Dr Smithson, 'they're going to fall!'

Lizzie and her friends, who had been standing either side of Kitchi as a sort of human blockade, scattered as the metal ladder came crashing down. A cacophony of sound filled the exhibition hall as the ladders smashed into the glass case in one corner. The crash and tinkle of breaking glass was followed by five loud thumps as one fossilised egg after the other dropped on to the hard floor of the museum.

The hairs on Lizzie's arms stood on end. She felt a prickling sensation at the back of her neck. *What's happening?* This was her moment. She could feel it in her bones. Walking over to the glass case she looked inside and noticed there the sixth egg was still there, trapped under the fallen ladders. Reaching inside she pulled it out. It had broken in two. She eased the two halves apart. At its heart lay a shiny, brown dimpled stone.

THE SACRED STONE

Lizzie looked at Kitchi and gave him a lopsided smile.

'I think I've found it,' she said.

'I think you have.'

In that moment time stood still. Lizzie glanced at the photograph of Barnum Brown on the wall by the broken display case.

So that's what you were trying to tell me all this time? The sacred stone was right here under my nose, but I couldn't see it.

She remembered that first smile. His appearance in the coal mine. All along he'd been trying to draw her back to the museum. And he had succeeded in the end. If she hadn't found the cavern and learned of the post-graduates' plan to steal the other T-Rex eggs, she wouldn't have been here now, trying to stop them.

***

Felipe and Sebastian's attempt at escape was thwarted by Maria who had jumped in the loaded jeep and driven it to Dr Smithson's house on the outskirts of Red Buck. They had no choice but to try and escape on foot. After several hours of walking in the dusty landscape they finally headed for the highway and slumped by the side of the road to await their fate. Dr Smithson had alerted the police who soon picked up the fugitives and took them into custody on a charge of attempted fossil theft under the Palaeontological Resources Preservation Act.

Dr Smithson went to see them in the local police station before they were taken to Macimanito to await trial.

'Why didn't you tell me the moment you found the eggs?' he asked them. 'Such a major discovery. You would have been feted all around North America as the first people to find a T-Rex embryo, yet you chose to be deceitful and try and steal the fossils.'

'What good is such glory here?' spat Felipe. 'We are South American. It is at home that our discovery should have been celebrated. It was my instinct, my nose that found these treasures. What good is my skill as a palaeontologist if I can't win recognition from my own people and bring the fossils back?'

Sebastian hung his head in shame. He had allowed himself to be manipulated by Felipe and had brought only disgrace on his father's good name.

'I am so sorry Eli,' he said. 'I was caught up in the plan and once the whole operation gained momentum it was difficult to stop. Forgive me.'

'It's too late for that Sebastian. I'll call your father and let him know what's happened. Thank goodness Maria, at least, had the good sense not to get involved in such a disgraceful scheme.'

'I wonder why that was,' said Felipe sarcastically as Eli left the room.

***

It was the final day of camp and an air of resignation hung over the students at breakfast. None of them was particularly looking forward to returning home and their everyday lives. The Badlands with its magical landscape, ancient creatures and hidden secrets had captured their hearts as well as their imaginations.

Dr Galloway sensed the deflation in his pupils' hunched postures, subdued conversation and unsmiling faces. He wasn't going to let camp end on anything but a positive note.

'Alright!' he said, standing up and clasping his hands in front of him. 'Now is the moment you've all been waiting for. Prize-giving!'

Lizzie looked at Josh and Sam, her eyes open wide. 'I thought that was a ruse by Felipe to keep us quiet about the eggs,' she whispered. 'I didn't realise there was going to be actual prizes awarded.'

Dr Galloway gestured to two of the teachers, who joined him at the end of the long dining table and started to lay out prizes on a trestle table behind him.

'The first award is for the best fossil project,' said Dr Galloway. 'The prize goes to … Callum, Jodi and Francesca for the cataloguing system they designed for small fossils.'

There was a ripple of applause as the award-winners left their seats and accepted their prizes, grinning broadly and high-fiving each other.

More awards followed, for the most enthusiastic fossil-hunter, the best presentation, the most meticulous fossil preparer and the best drawing of a dinosaur skeleton, among others.

'The final prize is for those student or students who have made the most contribution to the advancement of palaeontology,' said Dr Galloway.

'That's a fancy title,' whispered Sam.

'This is not one of our usual awards. It was suggested by Dr Smithson, curator of the Royal Clarkson Museum, who would like to say a few words.'

Dr Galloway gestured to Dr Smithson who had appeared earlier and sat at the opposite end of the tent.

'Thank you, Dr Galloway. First, I'd like to say how delighted I am to have seen you all enjoying yourselves over this last week. It has been wonderful to have you here and to witness such enthusiasm for scientific discovery among young people. Palaeontology is an exciting field to work in and I hope to see some of you back here one day studying for a career in this incredible branch of science.

'Now, to the real reason I'm here. You may have heard rumours that an extremely significant discovery was made very recently here in The Badlands. The circumstances are rather unusual and I'm not going to go into those today.

Suffice to say, three students among your group were heavily involved in bringing this unique fossil find to light.'

A murmur rose from the students who had no idea what he was talking about.

'Lizzie, Josh, Sam. Please step up to the front.' Dr Smithson gestured to the three friends, who rose from their seats and walked to where the curator was standing.

'These young people were implicit in uncovering the resting place of not one, not two, but six T-Rex eggs, only the second cluster ever to be found in this region ....'

'Wow!'

'That's incredible!'

'No way!'

Dr Smithson held up his hand to quell the hubbub.

'Not only that, but the first fossilised T-Rex embryo ever to be found ... in the world!' His voice rose to a crescendo.

There was spontaneous clapping from the students and teachers.

Lizzie and her friends couldn't help but smile at this, even though they were embarrassed to be singled out in this way.

'In recognition of this major contribution to palaeontology their names will be included on the plaque alongside the fossilised eggs and embryo in the museum. I'd also like to give them each a little something as a heartfelt thank you from myself and the museum.'

He handed them each a six-inch by three-inch square box that was surprisingly heavy.

'Well open them!' said Dr Galloway.

Lizzie opened hers first and gently pulled out a clear glass egg inside of which was embedded what looked like a bone.

'What is it?' she asked.

'Look on the bottom,' said Dr Smithson.

'Tail bone of a *bison antiquus*,' she read. 'Thank you so much.'

'An ancient ancestor of the buffalo,' he explained.

Josh and Sam had been given similar glass eggs with the bones of different prehistoric animals inside.

'Thank you once again Dr Smithson,' said Dr Galloway.

The curator and the three friends resumed their seats.

'Sadly, as you know, we will be leaving today to travel back to Macimanito,' continued Dr Galloway. 'The coach leaves at two o'clock sharp and there is plenty to do before then. I've pinned a sheet on the notice board with each of your duties. That's all!'

The students dispersed. Lizzie, Josh and Sam wandered back in the direction of their tents, each lost in their own thoughts.

As Lizzie was about to step into her tepee, she noticed Kitchi standing outside the camp entrance. He gestured for her to come over.

'Hi Kitchi!' she said. 'Look what I got.' She showed him the memento and explained what it was.

Kitchi smiled to himself. Very apt, he thought.

'You're not leaving with the others Lizzie. I have spoken to your mother and Dr Galloway. The Takoda people wish to thank you for finding their sacred stone. The ceremony is after nightfall. I will take you there.'

'Where to?'

'You'll see. It is a very special place. Not so far.'

THE ONE CALLED BUFFALO

Lizzie saw the fire first. The crescent moon cast no light on the darkened landscape. She and Kitchi had used flashlights to pick their way carefully along the banks of the Red Buck River and up on to an escarpment. Looking down into the coulee she could make out six figures sitting in a semicircle around a crackling fire. All around them huge, mushroom-shaped rocks leaned at odd angles as if they, too, were part of the gathering.

'This is the Takoda Tribe's sacred place,' said Kitchi. 'It is called the Badlands Guardian. Seen from the air it resembles a native chieftain's head in full headdress. Those rocks are hoodoos. The hard, sedimentary rock sits like a cap on top of the softer rock beneath which has been eroded by the wind and water. You are about to enter the ceremonial circle. Go now.'

Lizzie looked into Kitchi's eyes.

'Aren't you coming too.'

'I will be right behind you. Go down and stand the other side of the fire from the elders.'

Lizzie tentatively made her way down to the floor of the canyon and approached the gathering. In the glow from the fire she could see three men and three women with heavy blankets over their shoulders and heads slightly bowed. On the ground to one side was a crescent moon made of corn.

One of the elders gestured for her to come towards him. He held up a beaded bag.

'Reach inside. Don't be afraid. Take one out.'

Lizzie looked at the ancient face, white plaits falling either side of it. The eyes were so small and dark, so fixed on her own, she felt as though she were looking into the soul of an ancient civilisation. A past to which her connection was growing ever stronger.

She pulled out a card. It bore the picture of an eagle.

'Place it to your left,' said the elder. 'Now take another.'

The next card showed a dragonfly. She was instructed to place this at an angle slightly above the first. This process continued until she had created a semicircle of cards in front of her.

'These are seven of your nine totem animals,' said one of the female elders. 'You have chosen them using your intuition. They will guide you through your life. The other two, your Right Side and Left Side will walk with you at all times and may appear for you at a later time. One is your warrior spirit, your courage. The other is your nurturing side.

'The animal in the West,' she said, pointing to the card third from Lizzie's left, 'shows you the path to your goals. It is the mountain lion. It will teach you the power of leadership.

'Above,' one of the other elders said, indicating the card third from her right, 'gives you access to other dimensions. Here you have chosen the raven, the bringer of magic. It will give you the courage to enter the darkness, the void.'

'To your right is your Within animal. It protects your personal space and teaches you how to be faithful to your personal truths. You have chosen the white buffalo, the most sacred of animals to our people.'

Lizzie reached for the buffalo tooth around her neck. Her great grandfather's talisman, hers now. He must have chosen the buffalo too.

'You may have to honour another's pathway even if it brings you great sadness,' said the elder. 'This is part of the message the buffalo brings.'

'What about the other four animals?' Lizzie said quietly. She looked over her shoulder at Kitchi who sat in the darkness behind her. He gave her a reassuring nod.

'The eagle in the East is a reminder to take courage and soar beyond the horizon of what is visible. In the South you have chosen the dragonfly which brings change, and in the North the salmon, the keeper of wisdom that will guide you when to speak and when to listen. Below is the jaguar, the bringer of integrity and a compassionate heart. She will teach you the rewards of good deeds and impeccable behaviour.'

'But what does it all mean?'

'You are the one called buffalo, the chosen one. You must use the raven's magic to explore both visible and spiritual worlds for the good of others. The jaguar and eagle in you have already shown themselves in your courage and willingness to help the Takoda people. You saved the land under Macimanito for future generations. You found our sacred stone. Listen to the wisdom of the salmon and embrace the change the dragonfly brings. There will be some sadness along the way, but your totems will give you the strength to carry on. Your path will become clear.'

At that moment one of the female elders rose and walked over to Lizzie. Around her neck she placed a leather thong. Attached to it was the T-Rex tooth Lizzie had found in the coal mine after she saw Barnum's ghost.

'But how did you ...?' she said, turning to Kitchi.

'I found it among your things and asked Dr Smithson if you could keep it,' he said.

Oh no, thought Lizzie. She'd meant to hand it in and had completely forgotten.

'The Takoda wanted to bless it and return it to you as a talisman of your own.'

Lizzie felt the smooth surface of the tooth. Dinosaurs roamed the earth before humans. She wondered what qualities a Tyrannosaurus Rex totem might have. Ferocity perhaps!

'Thank you. Thank you so much.' She bowed her head at the elders.

'What happens now,' she whispered to Kitchi.

'Listen,' he replied.

A lilting melody echoed round the natural basin, filling the coulee with sound. The chanting seemed to take over all of Lizzie's senses. She entered a trance-like state. In her waking dream she saw forests with dark, winding tunnels and shadowy, menacing figures. She instinctively grasped her twin talismans for comfort. The moment the singing stopped she snapped out of it and shook her head to disperse the visions. Were they real or imagined, from the past, present or future? Only time would tell.

<<>>

ACKNOWLEDGEMENTS

The Alberta Badlands in Canada inspired the setting of 'The Sacred Stone', the second book in the Skyway Series. They form part of the Canadian Badlands which are one of the world's richest depositories of dinosaur bones. At their heart is the Royal Tyrrell Museum of Palaeontology, on which my Royal Clarkson Museum is loosely based. The attempted theft of fossils by postgraduate students from the museum is a complete fiction and no offence is intended to either students, their country of origin or the museum. Barnum Brown was an American palaeontologist, who lived from 1873 to 1963. Unlike the character in my story, however, he did not find the world's first Tyrannosaurus eggs in The Badlands. In real life he is credited with discovering the first documented remains of the T-Rex in Wyoming in 1900. He and his crew did spend time in Alberta, looking for fossils, and his dress-sense was as eccentric as I describe in my story. As far as I'm aware, he never met with members of Alberta's First Nations. The Badlands Passion Play does take place every year in July in the fabulous outdoor amphitheatre in Drumheller. I have had the privilege of watching performances there two years running. Many thanks to Darryl Reid who gave me permission to use his fabulous photo of Drumheller hoodoos against a backdrop of the aurora borealis as my front cover.

There are more than 600 indigenous groups in the USA and Canada. The Takoda is not one of them. In describing Lizzie's encounter with the elders of her tribe and the selection of her totem animals, I was guided by Jamie Sams & David Carson's wonderful book 'Medicine Cards', the contents of which were informed by the teaching of elders from various traditions of the native people of North America. The Badlands Guardian is a natural landform located in Alberta, which, from above, resembles a human head wearing an indigenous headdress.

Thank you Louise at 'Books Between Friends' in Calgary for taking me on as a volunteer during my two years living in the city, and thanks to TC, a fellow writer, for sharing your Thursdays with me.

ABOUT THE AUTHOR

Karen I Sage qualified as an electrical engineer and worked as a journalist and editor on trade magazines. She has a fascination with science and humankind's ingenuity, combined with a love of the natural world and a curiosity about the supernatural, which she hopes to share with children through her works of fiction.

Printed in Great Britain
by Amazon